MURDER IN SIENA

T. A. WILLIAMS

Boldwood

First published in Great Britain in 2023 by Boldwood Books Ltd.

Cover Design by Nick Castle

Cover Photography: Shutterstock

A CIP catalogue record for this book is available from the British Library.

Paperback ISBN 978-1-80483-247-9

Large Print ISBN 978-1-80483-248-6

Hardback ISBN 978-1-80483-249-3

Ebook ISBN 978-1-80483-245-5

Kindle ISBN 978-1-80483-246-2

Audio CD ISBN 978-1-80483-254-7

MP3 CD ISBN 978-1-80483-253-0

Digital audio download ISBN 978-1-80483-250-9

Boldwood Books Ltd
23 Bowerdean Street
London SW6 3TN
www.boldwoodbooks.com

To Mariangela who reads every word I write and helps me so much, and to Christina who likes a good whodunnit. With love as always.

PROLOGUE

FRIDAY EVENING

My first ever book signing was quite an occasion. My new publishers had somehow managed to take over one of the biggest bookshops in central London for a champagne reception – well, Prosecco really, but it tasted all right to me. The event took place at the end of March and it soon emerged that I was piggybacking on the official launch of a new romance by one of the best-known romantic fiction authors of the day, who also happened to be with the same publishers. The fact that I had never heard of her wouldn't have surprised my ex-wife. She used to complain that I didn't have a romantic bone in my body.

There were three of us: me with the first of my murder mysteries, a glamorous blonde woman who wrote kids' books, and the grey-haired, female author of the bestselling romances. The cover of her book featured a ginger-haired hunk stripped to the waist and boasting the sort of muscles that only come with hours in the gym and probably consumption of some dodgy substances. The title indicated that he was a duke who lived in a castle. This appeared to be haunted by a well-endowed young female ghost – or more probably a real woman wearing a diaphanous nightie.

Certainly, it looked very different from the menacing, dark red and black cover of my book, *Death Amid the Vines* – not my choice of title but I had been assured by my editor that this would be popular with crime aficionados. Considering that the publishers had been good enough to take me on as an untried new writer, who was I to complain?

We each had a table and it came as no surprise to find that the queue in front of the romance writer was a lot longer than mine. Also, her queue consisted almost exclusively of women, while mine was made up of an unexpectedly large contingent of my former workmates in the Metropolitan police, many of them male. As far as I could tell, the author of *Uncle Jack's Stories of Walter the Lonely Wolf* had attracted far fewer customers, but maybe that was because most of the kids were at home at this time of night. At my side was Tricia, my daughter, and she did a great job of making sure that I didn't keep people waiting and didn't drink too much Prosecco.

I was particularly touched to see that one of the first people in my line was none other than my one-time sergeant, now Inspector Wilson, from the days when I had been at Scotland Yard, and he was clutching no fewer than three copies of *Death Amid the Vines*. I stood up and greeted him warmly. He and I went way back and if this had been Italy, I would have hugged him but, seeing as we were British, we made do with a hearty handshake.

'Hi, Paul, it's good of you to come.'

'Hello, sir... Dan. Sorry, old habits.' He blushed and transferred his attention to Tricia. 'Good evening, Ms Armstrong.' His blushes increased and I remembered being told of a rumour going round the station a few years back that he had been sweet on her. She was now engaged to be married so he would appear to have missed his chance, but she shot him a winning smile all the same.

'Hi, Paul, and it's Tricia, remember? It's good to see you again.'

We chatted briefly and I asked him if he might be able to hang around for an hour or so until I finished my signing duties, after which we could go for a meal together. 'After all the help you've given me since I set up as a private investigator, buying you a good meal is the very least I can do.' There had been a number of occasions since settling in Italy almost two years earlier that I had called upon him for help, which he had generously provided.

He shook his head regretfully. 'Wish I could, but just now while I was waiting in the queue, I got a call. It looks like a fourteen-year-old has just stabbed a sixteen-year-old and I need to go and see what's what.'

I gave him a sympathetic smile in return. It sounded all too familiar and I was very pleased that resignation from the force and my move to Tuscany had distanced me from this sort of insanity. 'How is business? No shortage of villains or victims, I imagine.'

'Afraid not. Still, by the sound of it, you've been getting quite a bit of excitement over there in Italy, haven't you?'

'I'm being kept busy but, thankfully, most of my work these days is unfaithful husbands and jealous wives or vice versa. I'm told it's because the quality of Italian television is so poor, there's nothing else for them to do. I'm only here for tonight as I have work waiting for me back in Florence, but why don't you come over to Italy some time and see for yourself? I've got a spare room at my place that you're welcome to have, and that way you can meet my new best friend, Oscar.'

'That's the big, black Labrador you sent me a photo of? Thanks for the offer; I might well take you up on it when I manage to get some time off.' He glanced at his watch. 'Sorry, but now I need to head off. Can you sign one book to Maureen – that's my mum – and one to George, my uncle. The other one's for me.'

I did as requested and added a note above my signature on his copy saying,

To the best detective in the business from an old copper and friend.

And he definitely qualified on all counts.

In fact, it was probably just as well that he hadn't been able to stick around as I found that the signing took almost two hours. It was past eight o'clock when the line in front of my desk finally dried up and one of the shop assistants came to tell me that they had closed the doors. There were still a dozen or so hopefuls queuing in front of the romance lady so I wandered over to see how the children's author had got on. On the rare occasions when I had been able to look up from my work, I hadn't seen many people where she was, but she greeted me with a big smile all the same.

'Hi there, Dan. Or is that your *nom de plume*? I'm Uncle Jack – although my real name's Freja Blomqvist. Do I look like an Uncle Jack?'

The answer to that one was no, unless Uncle Jack had a taste for smart women's dresses and gold jewellery. Freja/Jack was a very good-looking woman probably in her forties, with a cascade of pale-blonde hair that perfectly framed what was a pretty perfect face. She spoke excellent English with just a hint of a Scandinavian accent.

'Hi, Uncle Jack, but it's hard trying to think of you as my uncle. Good to meet you, and yes, at least my name's my own even if the title of my book isn't. What about you? Do you at least get to choose your own title?'

Freja nodded. 'Walter the wolf is all my own invention. Did I hear that you used to be a detective?'

'That's right; here in London, but I now live and work in Italy. Ever been there?'

'A few times and funnily enough, I'll be there again in just over a week. My day job is working in the zoology department at Stockholm University and I'll be taking part in a symposium in Italy for a few days.' She gave me another of those alluring smiles and I had to remind myself that I had a wonderful girlfriend waiting for me back in Florence. 'I don't think I've sold more than a dozen books tonight, but six o'clock in the evening in central London probably wasn't the best time to bring in the mums and their kids. How about you? How's the book selling?'

We chatted for a while and I took a liking to this woman who was obviously eminent in her own field as well as having the imagination to branch out into a second career as an author.

Before long, the last of the romance books were finally signed and my editor, Suzanne, appeared and took me by the elbow while Tricia went off to call her fiancé. 'That was great, Dan. You managed to bring in a good number of readers. There's somebody here who's been waiting to see you. She's a journalist and she says she knows you. Wouldn't it be great if she did an article about you?' She glanced across at Freja 'We'll all have time for a good chat over dinner.'

I bade farewell to Freja/Uncle Jack just as her editor, a mumsy-looking lady with half-lens glasses balanced on the end of her nose, arrived to take her under her wing. As Suzanne led me across to meet the journalist, she reassured me that the company were very pleased with sales of *Death Amid the Vines* so far – it had only been out for three weeks – and outlined the plans they had to promote it to even better things. This all came as a great relief as, since it was my first ever book, I had had no idea how it would be received.

Across the shop floor, sitting on a tiny chair in the children's books department, was a familiar face, and seeing her brought a host of memories flooding back – few of them pleasant, but that wasn't her fault. As a crime reporter, Jess Barnes had covered some of the goriest murders in the capital over the last twenty years or so and I had lost count of the number of times I had bumped into her in the less salubrious areas of the city, where gangland violence had repeatedly shown its face. She jumped up as she caught sight of me and surprised me by rushing over and giving me a hug and a smacker of a kiss. Seeing my surprise, she stepped back and grinned.

'It's all right, Chief Inspector, I'm allowed to kiss you now that you've retired.'

I smiled back. 'If I'd realised that was what was holding you back, I'd have retired years ago. It's good to see you again, Jess, and it's just Dan these days, not Chief Inspector. How are you?'

'I'm fine, thanks.'

I rummaged around in my fifty-six-year-old memory banks and managed to come up trumps. 'How are Keith and the twins? All well, I hope.'

'All good, now come and sit down and tell me all about how you've become a famous author.' She glanced across at my editor, who was looking on with interest. 'How long have I got him for? Ten minutes? Okay, I'll make it quick.'

I perched down on one of the kiddies' chairs opposite her with my knees under my chin and she rattled off a series of questions, which I did my best to answer while she scribbled in incredibly fast shorthand. I told her about my move to Tuscany and my new venture as a private investigator, but I avoided mentioning my divorce. The trouble with journalists is that they will publish anything and I had learnt over the years to weigh my words when talking to them, even if they were old trusties like Jess. She asked me about my book and surprised me by producing a copy she had bought and asking me to sign it for her. As I ran through a rough outline of the story and how I had come up with it, part of my brain was still reminiscing about my time in the force. They had been busy times, sometimes exciting, sometimes desperately sad, but I had absolutely no regrets about making the big move to Italy and I told her so.

Finally, as Suzanne began to get restless, Jess concluded the interview and asked if she could take a photo of me holding the book. She took several on her phone and this also reminded me of the days when journalists like her had been accompanied by photographers carrying bags full of equipment. Now the resolution you can get from a smartphone is every bit good enough for the front pages of the papers. I stood up to shake hands and she gave me another kiss and told me she was hopeful she could use her many contacts to get the article into one of the big newspapers, maybe in their weekend issue. She grinned.

'When the bad boys see you're now writing whodunnits, they'll be quaking in their boots, wondering if you've written about them.'

'The advice to authors is to write about what you know, but if I wrote about some of the stuff you and I've seen, the books would probably be banned. You take care, Jess. Great to see you again.'

Dinner was in a swanky Indian restaurant just around the corner from the bookshop and I was delighted at the choice. I love Tuscany and I love Italian food, but I sometimes find myself dreaming of having a good curry, and that night I certainly got my wish. I was sitting with Suzanne on one side of me and Tricia on the other, while Freja from Sweden was opposite us with her editor. The famous romance author was at the head of the table alongside one of the big bosses, but she generously included me in the conversation from time to time. She asked me to what extent my background in the police had helped my writing and, after explaining that it had been immensely helpful, I couldn't help asking her what experience she had of red-headed aristocrats with no shirts. I sensed a frisson run around the table, but she was up to the challenge.

'In my dreams, Dan. That's the thing about writing, so much of it is imagination.' Then, to my surprise, she threw me a decidedly saucy wink. 'But if you feel like ripping off your shirt here at the table, don't let me stop you. It'll be good research, I'm sure.' For a moment, my eyes met those of Freja/Uncle Jack and I saw her nodding vigorously and I hastily transferred my attention to my daughter. One thing was for sure: my shirt was staying firmly on my back.

Altogether it was an enjoyable evening and I came out of it beginning to believe there might be a future for me as a writer, although a quick check of my messages back in my hotel room reminded me that I couldn't give up the day job. Yet another suspicious wife was desperate to see me when I got back to Tuscany.

Dan Armstrong, Private Investigator, had work to do.

1

THE FOLLOWING FRIDAY MORNING

'We turn left here, I think.'

'You think?' I did my best to keep most of the scepticism out of my voice but Anna still must have heard it.

'If you could see the directions I've been given, it's a miracle we're anywhere near the place.' She waved a piece of brown paper at me, on which I could just about make out pencil marks. 'It's like I told you, Dan, these people are still living in the Stone Age. The paper it's written on is recycled wrapping paper and it's a wonder they managed to find an envelope so they could send the letter through the post. From what I've heard of them, they probably do most of their communication by jungle drums or smoke signals.'

I could hear the frustration in her voice and I was quick to calm her – and me – as I turned off the lane onto a dusty, bumpy track between an overgrown vineyard on my left and an equally run-down olive grove on the right. Considering the manicured rows of vines we had been driving through to get here, it came as quite a surprise to find that the owners of this land were letting it stand idle. This part of Tuscany was one of the richest wine producing areas in Italy, if not Europe, and it was rare to find wasted space.

I shot her a reassuring glance. 'Don't worry, sweetheart, we'll find them. I must say, from the build-up, I'm looking forward to meeting these people. I'm just amazed that a couple of New Age hippies managed to collect the money together to buy themselves a house in Tuscany in the first place. Let's face it, this isn't the cheapest area of Italy.'

'Who knows? Rosanna in the art department who gave me their letter says she's never met them but they're sort of vaguely friends of friends of hers. Maybe Reiner Schladming's father was a wealthy man and they inherited money from him. Or maybe it came from his wife. It'll be interesting to find out.'

'And Reiner Schladming is... German?'

'Originally Austrian, apparently, but Rosanna's friend said he spent years living in the States before coming over here to make a fresh start.'

I looked around at the tree-covered hills and unspoilt country-side and had to admit that Tuscany was a pretty good place if you wanted to make a fresh start. After all, that was what I had done, although none of my relatives had been kind enough to leave me a fortune.

The track passed through a clump of pine trees and then turned sharply to the right and climbed towards a building just visible on top of a low rise ahead of us, sheltered by a pair of abso-lutely massive umbrella pines. Cypress trees lined the drive and as we approached the old stone farmhouse, it was almost like being in a *Visit Tuscany* advert. The house itself looked as if it had always been there, made out of the wonderful honey-coloured local stone and with an arched loggia to one side from where I felt sure there would be spectacular views back down the valley again. Yes, not a bad place to live at all.

When we arrived in front of the old farmhouse, an elderly sheepdog emerged through the fly curtain strung across the front door and started barking. This sparked movement from behind me as my own dog decided that it was his duty to reply to this greeting, and he almost deafened us as he did so.

'Oscar, for crying out loud!' I came to a halt and swivelled round in my seat to find the Labrador with his front paws on top of the back seat as he responded enthusiastically to the other dog's welcome – or lack of. 'Oscar, shush!'

Fortunately, at that moment, the owner emerged from the house and the sheepdog, satisfied that he had done his duty, stopped barking and sauntered across to pee on the front wheel of my car. Convinced that he had won the vocal battle, Oscar gave one final triumphant woof and then, mercifully, obeyed the command to be quiet. The ensuing silence – albeit accompanied by ringing in our ears – was a blessed relief. I shot an apologetic look across towards Anna. 'Sorry about that. You know Oscar; he always gets excited when other dogs start barking at him.'

She gave me a smile in return. Now that her navigation skills had been crowned with success, she could afford to be magnanimous. 'Don't worry, it's only natural. At least the good news is that Oscar's a very friendly dog. There's no way he would start attacking another dog, is there?'

'Good Lord, no. He's far too lazy for that. Well, shall we go and introduce ourselves?'

'As long as the sheepdog doesn't mind.' Anna sounded hesitant and the dog's master must have sensed her uncertainty as he gave a sharp command, unintelligible to me but which was instantly recognised by the sheepdog, who immediately trotted back to sit primly at the man's feet.

I glanced back at Oscar and pointed. 'See, Oscar, that's what good dogs do.'

He just wagged the end of his tail. We both knew that was never going to happen.

We opened the doors and climbed out of the car. The air was clean and fresh out here and the only sound, now that the dogs had stopped barking, was the clucking of hens somewhere around the back of the old building. I left Oscar in the car for now and followed Anna across to the man by the house. Clearly, she had been expected, seeing as he extended his hand to greet her, but the expression on his face wasn't much more welcoming than that of his sheepdog.

'Good morning, you must be Doctor Galardo.' His Italian wasn't great and she instinctively replied in English – which she speaks like a native after having lived and worked in the UK for years.

'Good morning, Reiner, it's lovely to meet you. I'm Anna.' She shot him a beaming smile, which wasn't reciprocated, before pointing in my direction. 'This is my friend, Dan. He's British but, like you, he lives here in Tuscany now.'

I walked over to him and we shook hands, although I sensed reluctance on his part. It occurred to me that maybe he had chosen to live out here in the back of beyond for a reason – like detesting his fellow man, for example. Nevertheless, I followed Anna's example and plastered on a friendly smile but, once again, got nothing back from him. 'Good to meet you, Reiner.' The old sheepdog surveyed us suspiciously from his master's feet but made no attempt to greet us in his turn. I indicated my car where Oscar's big, black nose was pressed up against the window, steaming up the glass, his tail wagging hopefully. 'Shall I leave the dog in the car?'

'No, bring him in by all means.' As we spoke of animals, the Austrian's stony expression momentarily softened. 'Attila won't mind.' There then followed an awkward silence before he remembered why we were here. 'You'd better come inside.' Bizarrely, although he had a strong Germanic accent when he spoke Italian, his English was delivered with a very convincing American accent.

The expression on the sheepdog's face was anything but welcoming but I went back to release Oscar anyway and hoped that Attila wouldn't live up to his bloodthirsty name. Fortunately, to my surprise, after a cursory sniff, the two dogs studiously ignored each other. Reiner led us in through the fly curtain – although why they needed a fly curtain right at the beginning of April was a mystery to me – and into a huge living room, which encompassed kitchen, dining room, lounge and, by the look of it, artist's studio. There was a strong smell of oil paint and linseed oil as we walked in and its source appeared to be a tall, frighteningly pale woman with a cascade of grey hair hanging almost to her waist. She was wearing bright-green clown's trousers, gathered at the ankles, which reinforced the artistic look. Reiner, on the other hand, looked like a throwback to Victorian days with a collarless, white shirt, black waistcoat and Abraham Lincoln beard. His wife came across to say hello with half a dozen paintbrushes held in the fingers of her right hand. She at least managed to produce a genuine-looking smile.

'Good morning, my name's Suzy. You've come about the mural, haven't you?' She, too, sounded convincingly American.

Anna confirmed that was indeed why we were here and we duly shook her free left hand. She waved vaguely towards the chairs around the kitchen table, on one of which a massive, ginger cat was snoozing, apparently oblivious to our arrival. I glanced at Oscar, who hadn't yet spotted the cat, anticipating trouble when he did. Suzy must have realised my concern as she shook her head.

'Don't worry about Gretel. She won't bother your dog.'

It was their cat, not my dog, I was worried about, but I

suspended my disbelief and looked on as Oscar wandered across to the chairs, stopped dead when he saw the cat and did a double take. Just as I was expecting the scene to erupt into a wall-of-death chase around the room, the cat opened first one and then, reluctantly, the other eye, stretched languorously and subjected the Labrador to an expression that quite plainly indicated that there was only one boss around here and her name was Gretel. To my surprise, Oscar made no attempt to disturb the status quo and came across to my side, where he gave me a look that could easily be translated as, *What the hell just happened?* I gave him a pat on the head and we sat down around the table.

Suzy murmured something in German to her husband and he nodded dutifully before making an attempt at observing accepted norms of behaviour. I could see the effort it was costing him and this added weight to my conviction that he had opted out of normal society for a reason. 'Coffee, tea, schnapps?'

I've never been a great one for the hard stuff, and eleven o'clock in the morning was definitely far too early to start, even if I was on holiday for the next five days, so I thanked Reiner for the offer of booze and just asked for a coffee, as did Anna. Our reluctant host turned on his heel and went over to a wonderful old relic of a cast-iron stove and started fiddling about, producing a cloud of smoke in the process. Clearly, it was wood-powered. The two ladies settled down to talk about the mural and I listened in.

Reiner and Suzy had contacted the university to ask for an expert to give an assessment of an ancient mural found on one of the walls of this six-hundred-year-old property. Anna teaches medieval and Renaissance history at Florence University and, seeing as she and I had been coming down here to the Tuscan hills south of Siena for an early spring break, she had volunteered to call in on the Austrian/American couple. After a few moments, the two ladies got up and went off to view the mural but I felt I should stay with Reiner – and keep an eye on my dog in case the cat decided to assault him. I tried a bit of conversation.

'How long have you lived over here in Tuscany, Reiner?'

The reply was a long time coming and when it did, it sounded as if it was delivered unwillingly. 'Four years now.'

Undeterred, I tried again. 'Where were you living before?'

I had a long wait while he fussed with the stove and set a well-used coffee pot on top of it. Finally he glanced at me over his shoulder. 'New York City.'

Clearly the man was not a natural communicator but, having started, I did my best to carry on at least an attempt at conversation.

'Wow, must have been quite a change.' This elicited no response so I took one last stab at it. 'Do you have much land here?' This at least produced an almost immediate reply and he turned towards me.

'Twenty hectares.'

That sounded like a lot to me. 'Do you farm the land?'

'Only a very small portion of it. I'm too old for the digging these days. I have trouble with my back.' As if regretting this unusually long reply, he turned away and started rooting around in a cupboard for cups.

'Couldn't you get somebody to help you?'

'I'm happier on my own and, besides, I find it patronising to employ another human being. That just demeans them. No, anything that needs doing, I try to do myself.'

I raised my eyebrows at that. From his appearance, I reckoned he wouldn't see seventy again and, although he looked healthy enough, he didn't look particularly strong. What would he do, I wondered, when his roof started leaking or his private sewage system filled up? But that wasn't my business – thankfully. I threw out a practical suggestion and immediately regretted it. 'Haven't you got a tractor or a rotovator or something?'

He straightened up and came back across to the table where he stood glowering down at me, an expression of extreme distaste on his face. 'Machines!' He almost spat the word out. 'That's all the world seems to want nowadays: machines. Bigger, noisier and ever more polluting machines. More CO_2, more destruction.' He fixed me with his odd, pale-grey eyes. 'We're destroying the planet, and nobody seems prepared to do anything about it.' He turned and went off to the stove where the coffee pot was already steaming, leaving me pondering his words.

I glanced around and couldn't help noticing that the light hanging above the table was an old candelabra with six genuine wax candles on it. There was no TV, no fridge, as far as I could see, no radiators, and the porcelain light switches on the walls looked antediluvian. Anna hadn't been joking when she had said these people belonged to the Stone Age. Mind you, if they could exist without power and without modern conveniences, they were at least doing their bit for the planet, but I didn't envy them their spartan life. Did they even have hot water? If not, then how did he get his shirt so white? I waited until Reiner came over with the coffees and then brought up the subject again.

'But surely some modern machines are essential. What about a car? How do you go into town to do the shopping?'

'I walk – it's only five kilometres – or if there's heavy stuff to carry, I take the horse and cart.'

'Does that mean you don't have a car?'

He shuddered and shook his head emphatically. 'God forbid. No, I certainly do *not* have a car. We left all those inventions of the Devil behind when we said goodbye to the States.'

I wondered idly how the two of them had got over here. It's a long way to swim from New York. 'What about travelling further afield? Going to Siena, say?' Siena was about twenty-five kilometres to the north.

'If I absolutely have to go there, I take the bus.'

'But what if one of you is ill?'

'Do you know how long it is since either of us last saw a doctor? Over thirty years. We don't trust doctors and we don't trust scientists. It's scientists who're destroying the planet.'

By now I had worked out that Reiner had a seriously low opinion of modern technology and those responsible for developing and delivering it, but I wondered if he would stand by his principles if he or his wife were taken seriously ill. Still, it was impressive to see people prepared to practise what they preached, even though he certainly wasn't the warmest of characters. I sipped my surprisingly good coffee and did the English thing of turning the conversation to the less contentious issue of the weather – or so I thought. Seconds later, I was on the receiving end of a diatribe on the effects of greenhouse gases on the world and how climate change was about to doom humanity.

Fortunately, his flow was interrupted by the return of the two ladies and an invitation from Anna to come and view the mural. I was only too happy to accompany her out along a freezing cold corridor and I noticed that Oscar seemed equally happy to distance himself from the cat and follow us. Anna led the way to a small, low-ceilinged room where the end wall contained a remarkable depiction of the crucifixion, about six feet by six feet square. It was beautifully painted and in surprisingly good condition, assuming it really was as old as the house. I've always had a suspicious streak so I had to ask.

'Stunningly good if it's original. What's your verdict? Medieval or a later date?'

'Almost certainly original, I would say, but without taking a sample of the paint to study, it's hard to be 100 per cent sure.'

'What's involved with taking a paint sample? Doesn't it damage the painting?'

'The quantity I would need would hardly be missed, but Suzy was very firm in her refusal to let me touch it. Her husband forbids it; he doesn't trust me.' From Anna's tone, it was clear how she felt about that, and I didn't blame her. Reiner was quite something. A voice from behind made us both turn round. It was Suzy herself.

'It's not that he doesn't trust you personally, Anna.' Her tone was apologetic and I noticed that she kept her voice low, presumably so that her words wouldn't carry through to Reiner in the kitchen. 'He just doesn't want anything of ours ending up in a laboratory.'

In little more than a whisper, she went on to apologise again and express her regret at her husband's stand on this, but it was clear that she knew there was no way she would ever be able to sway him. As far as Reiner was concerned, scientists, of whatever type, were the spawn of Satan. End of story.

Altogether, we spent almost an hour with the two of them and Suzy gave us a conducted tour of their property from the charming old loggia with, as I had expected, a spectacular view over the surrounding countryside, to a spine-chillingly – literally – bare bathroom. This had a suspicious smell that indicated to me that the moment when Reiner was going to need the help of a drainage engineer was probably well overdue.

Outside, we met Boris, their handsome black horse with a distinctive white face, and admired the sturdy cart that went with him, as well as the manually operated pump that was their only source of water. I was impressed with the couple's resilience, but knowing that I was spending the next five nights in a comfortable hotel appealed to me a whole lot more.

It came as no surprise to find that Reiner steadfastly refused Anna's requests to allow some of her other colleagues to come and study the mural in more detail. Whether it was a genuine medieval painting or not, one thing was clear: this crucifixion scene would remain unseen by anybody, at least as long as this antisocial man lived here.

When the time came to leave, all three of us – and I'm including my unusually subdued dog after his encounter with a cat who clearly didn't understand the mechanics of the normal feline-canine relationship – were only too happy to get back into the car and head off down the hill, although I was sure Anna must be feeling sorry for Suzy just as I was. It was quite clear to me that, in spite of his wife's best efforts, Reiner had deliberately made the decision to separate the two of them from the rest of humanity. I rather got the impression that the rest of humanity wouldn't miss him.

2

FRIDAY AFTERNOON

'If you ever feel you're having a rough time, spare a thought for these little guys.'

I looked down and followed the direction of Virgilio's pointing finger. There, at the edge of the track just ahead of us, were two shiny black dung beetles, diligently rolling a ball of fresh manure twice their size towards the long grass. The track between the vines was made up of sand and gravel and the animals struggled to roll their precious find over obstacles almost imperceptible to the human eye but no doubt immensely daunting to these insects little bigger than my fingernails.

'There were times back in the old days when I felt like that.' I stopped and watched as the tiny insects completed their Herculean task and my mind went back to my days at Scotland Yard. 'Getting called out of bed in the middle of the night to deal with a murder scene like something out of a horror movie and then working an eighteen-hour shift, before going home to find the cat lying in my spot on the sofa and my wife not talking to me.' I looked up at him and shook my head ruefully. 'Yes, there were times when I would have envied these little chaps.'

Virgilio reached over and clapped me on the shoulder. 'But that's all over now, isn't it?' He glanced over his shoulder to where Anna and his wife, Lina, were following us up the track, delayed by my dog's insistent and repeated demands for them to throw his stick for him to retrieve. When I say *his* stick, I don't mean that he has a special one. For him, any old stick will do as long as somebody's prepared to throw it for him to go and fetch, thus allowing him to prove that he has inherited the retriever gene as well as the well-known Labrador gluttony gene. Virgilio beamed at me. 'No more midnight calls and no more unhappy wife. What more could you ask for?'

'What more indeed?' My eyes flicked back to Anna, who was deep in conversation with Lina about something, and I felt myself smiling. The divorce was history now so hopefully those unhappy times had passed. My eyes swept on across our surroundings. On both sides of us were neat rows of vines, already starting to show the first green shoots as warm spring sunshine banished the frosts of what had been a hard winter here in Tuscany. Beyond the vines, the ground rose steeply and the slopes were covered in dense woodland that stretched all the way up to the tops of the hills that framed the vineyards around this isolated country hotel. As the crow flies, we weren't far from Reiner and Suzy's house or the historic city of Siena but it felt like another world. Yes, it could hardly have been more different from the grimy suburbs of London.

Thoughts of London reminded me of the book signing the previous week and I hoped Suzanne hadn't been exaggerating when she had told me how pleased they were with the way sales of the book were going. It had been good to meet my first ever editor for the first time after communicating only by email before, and I had been pleasantly surprised and delighted to see so many of my old colleagues on the force who had been prepared to come out to support me. It had also been great to spend a day with Tricia again, but we've always been close. As for her mother, she hadn't come down to London for the event and I didn't blame her. Our relationship was all over now and we had both moved on. I glanced back towards Anna again. Yes, I could genuinely say I had moved on as well, and I was glad I had done.

'Now, what on earth do you think those two are doing?'

Virgilio's voice drew my attention back to the track ahead of us. About a hundred yards further along, two people were squatting down, studying what looked from here like a pile of dog poo in the middle of the track. The closer we got to them, the more obvious it became that the object of their attention was indeed what is euphemistically referred to as canine by-product. One of the less appealing traits of my dog is his keen interest in such things. Although I do my bit by picking up after him, I have never felt the urge to crouch down and study the stuff as intently as the two people ahead of us.

As we neared them, I realised to my considerable surprise that the woman and I knew each other. She looked up, did a double take as she realised who I was, and leapt to her feet.

'Hi, Dan, fancy meeting you here.' To my acute discomfort – seeing as my girlfriend was only a little way behind – she came rushing up to me, flung her arms around my neck and kissed me – and I don't mean just a quick air kiss somewhere near the cheeks. This was a real smacker. 'This must be fate!'

'Freja, how amazing.' I could see Virgilio giving me a quizzical look and I did my best to sound as if being kissed by gorgeous blondes was an everyday occurrence. I'm sure Humphrey Bogart would have done it more convincingly. 'What brings you here?' I almost asked her why she was sniffing dog poo but decided to leave that for now.

In fact, thinking about it, it wasn't that surprising to find her here. Presumably she was one of the delegates at the symposium currently taking place in the hotel's conference facility. I thought back to what she had told me in London. She had said she was a zoologist and, from what I had seen on the posters and banners around the place, the symposium was all about ecology. No doubt she was here on the strength of her zoological background. The symposium had all but taken over the hotel and we'd been lucky to get just about the last two remaining rooms when Virgilio had suggested this long weekend break in the country.

Freja's red-haired companion was probably in his early or mid-forties, as she was, but he was nowhere near as glamorous. He was looking very intense and businesslike and, crouching suspiciously close to the pile of dog poo, he could hardly have been described as particularly appealing. On the other hand, Freja's appearance only confirmed the impression I had gained of her in London. Today, she was wearing a tank top, shorts and dusty desert boots, but with her long, blonde hair and her suntanned legs – on display even now at the beginning of April – she had to be one of the most beautiful scientists I had ever seen.

The man looked up but made no effort to stand up or move. Clearly, his faecal investigation was serious. In fact, he was looking quite defensive.

'Please keep your dog away. This is important.' He made no attempt to speak Italian. I had already noted that the symposium was being conducted in English. His accent sounded mid or eastern European, maybe from Poland or somewhere around there, although with his mop of ginger hair, he could have been from almost anywhere in Europe.

By now, the others were catching us up and I reached out to grab Oscar by the collar and restrain him from quite literally poking his nose in where he wasn't wanted. Although Anna said nothing, I felt sure she must have noticed Freja's enthusiastic greeting to me and I could sense a certain amount of tension in the air, so I was quick to make the introductions in English. 'Anna, this is my fellow author, Freja.' I couldn't remember her surname, something Swedish beginning with B. 'She writes kids' books under the name Uncle Jack. We met last week at the book signing.'

Anna stepped forward and held out a welcoming hand. 'Hello, Freja, I'm Anna. Dan told me the book signing was a lot of fun.'

The Swede smiled back. 'It was certainly a lot different from this.' She waved her hand towards her colleague and the pile of poo.

I felt I had to ask. 'Is there something special about this pile of dog poo?'

The ginger-haired man gave me the sort of look teenagers give their parents when they mistake Jay-Z for Eminem, or some similar heinous demonstration of ignorance.

'*Canis lupus italicus.* These are not canine droppings.'

In case we were still uncertain, Freja translated. 'These are wolf faeces and they're fresh. There must be a pack nearby.'

'Wolf faeces? There are wolves here in Tuscany?' This was news to me.

She nodded. 'Yes, indeed, there are probably more wolves in Tuscany than in any other part of Italy or, indeed, any part of western Europe. At the last count, there were over a hundred packs in this region alone.'

'And a pack consists of how many wolves?'

'Anything from two to about ten, depending on the time of year.' Seeing my awestruck expression, she nodded. 'Yes, that adds up to quite a few wolves.'

Virgilio's wife, Lina, had been going to evening classes to

improve her English but it wasn't yet up to fully understanding complicated English and I heard Anna translating for her benefit. As the message sank in, I heard a sharp intake of breath. Lina then came up with the question that was already on my lips and I repeated it in English to the two scientists.

'Are they dangerous?'

The man gave me a long-suffering look. From his expression, I imagined he must get asked this quite a lot. 'Not to humans. You're quite safe. There have been no reported wolf attacks on humans in western Europe for over fifty years. Wolves see us as a threat and they tend to stay clear of humans as a result.'

I pointed to Oscar. 'And what about my dog?'

'He's probably a bit more at risk. There were reports of a dog being killed not that long ago up in the Italian Alps but, to be honest, it's more likely that a friendly female wolf might seek him out as a sexual partner.'

I glanced down and wagged my finger at him. 'Now, don't you go getting any ideas, Oscar. If you see a she-wolf, however good-looking she is, you stay clear. All right? The last thing I need is a jealous male wolf tearing you limb from limb.' In response, he wagged his tail, but I wasn't convinced he understood the potential severity of the situation.

We left the two scientists to their work and we carried on with our walk. As we did so, it would be fair to say that all four of us spent quite a lot of the time scanning the surrounding vegetation for any sign of a pack of marauding carnivores but fortunately, we saw none. By this time I had remembered that Freja's surname was Blomqvist and I told the others more about her and her books and we all marvelled at the synchronicity of the two of us finding ourselves here at the same time. I had already recounted some of my experiences in London with them over lunch and now that

Virgilio had met the Swedish scientist, he made it clear that he shared my impression of her.

'If I'd had a science teacher who looked like that, I would have studied a whole lot harder at school.'

I studiously kept my eyes off the two ladies and did my best to look as if I hadn't noticed Freja's appearance but Anna, who knew me so well by now, wasn't buying it.

'You didn't tell me Uncle Jack was so beautiful, Dan. In fact, I don't seem to remember you telling me that Uncle Jack was female. I wonder why that was.'

'Oh, you know, I didn't think it was important. After all, it's her writing that counts, not her looks.' I felt a cold, wet nose prod me on the leg and I looked down. From the expression on my dog's face, he wasn't buying it either so I was quick to produce my alibi. 'I was there with Tricia, so I wasn't really concentrating on the others.'

Anna reached up and gave me a peck on the cheek. She was grinning. 'For somebody who's spent his life interrogating people, you're terrible when the boot's on the other foot. Even Oscar could see that she's a beautiful woman but so what? You're with me, not her.'

I kissed her back. 'And I couldn't be happier.' And I meant it.

Gradually, as the track curled round and began to lead us back through the vineyards towards the hotel once more, we returned to enjoying what was turning out to be a most relaxing short holiday after a busy winter.

For Virgilio, a detective inspector in the Florence murder squad, the winter had brought the usual crop of crimes of passion, drug-related homicides and rampages by deranged killers. Although I was now a private investigator, he and I had become close friends and I had heard about most, if not all, of the worst of them and had helped out on a number of occasions. As for me, it had been a fairly unremarkable few months workwise, but a combination of jealous spouses, suspicious employers, and social media spats that had got out of hand had kept me busy and had provided a welcome boost to my bank account. In fact, things had been going so well that I was beginning to wonder whether I should think about expanding the business. Even just being able to take these five days off had been tricky and if it carried on like this, I knew I would need another pair of hands. All things considered, Dan Armstrong, Private Investigations, was doing pretty well.

On a personal level also, I couldn't complain either. Meeting Anna had been the best thing that had happened to me for years, and we had been drawing ever closer. The little house in the hills just outside Florence that I had bought the previous year was now very comfortable. The plumber had finished installing an effective central heating system back in the autumn, and my dog and I had been cosy over the winter without a trace of ice on the inside of the bathroom window – unlike the previous year. I breathed deeply and allowed myself a contented sigh. Yes, life was good once more.

The hotel that Virgilio had chosen for our early spring break, Hotel dei Boschi Idilliaci was in the hills just to the south of Siena, less than an hour's drive from my home near Florence. Although I'd been living here in Tuscany for almost two years now, I didn't know Siena very well and I was looking forward to visiting it again over the next few days. With my own personal medieval guide, this promised to be instructive as well as enjoyable. As for this area, it proved yet again just how wild Tuscany is once you get away from the famous historical towns and cities. Over the past months, Oscar and I had explored the countryside near Florence and had discovered kilometres of stunning countryside filled with vineyards and olive groves, accessed along the famous *strade bianche* – literally the 'white roads' because of the colour of the gravel. Here in the area around the hotel, there were vineyards, but also vast expanses of unspoilt woodland that hadn't changed at all in millennia. Yes, as a place to live, Tuscany certainly took some beating.

And, by the sound of it, a pack of wolves shared that opinion.

3

FRIDAY LATE AFTERNOON / EVENING

At the end of our walk, we sat down on the terrace outside the hotel and had afternoon tea. Well, I had tea and the three Italians had coffee, but each to his or her own. As far as Oscar at my feet was concerned, he didn't care what the humans drank as long as he got at least one of the little complimentary biscuits. Out here in the early April sunlight, it was far from cold, although the overnight temperatures were still dropping to single figures. I stretched my legs and sat back with my cup of English Breakfast tea – it was five o'clock in the afternoon, but so what?

As I sat there, I witnessed an intriguing scene. A bit further along the terrace, a man was leaning on the balustrade looking out over the formal garden as he sipped what looked like a cup of tea. He was side on to me and I could see a badge attached to a lanyard around his neck, which told me he was one of the symposium participants, who had popped out for a break. Instinctively, I noted that he was probably in his forties, of average height and weight, and he had a neatly trimmed, light-brown, hipster beard. As I looked on, an olive-skinned man around the same age with a luxuriant head of stylish, black hair came out through the glass doors and headed straight for the tea drinker. I immediately recognised him from lunchtime. I had mentally christened him Casanova after seeing him embracing no fewer than three different women in the space of half an hour – and when I say embracing, I mean snogging. Clearly he liked the ladies and it would appear that they liked him.

He marched across to the other man and when he got to him, he jabbed him sharply on the shoulder with his finger so that the hipster turned towards him, spilling some of his tea in the process. At that point, the dark-haired man unleashed a stream of what sounded like invective in a language with which I was unfamiliar.

What was interesting was the reaction of his opponent. A look of what could have been guilt appeared on his face for a split second, closely followed by an expression of distaste as he waved the other man away as if swatting an annoying insect. This appeared to do little to calm his aggressor, who reached forward and grabbed him by the lapels of his jacket, looking as if he were about to explode. The tea in the other man's cup took another hit and dripped onto both pairs of shoes. The two men were about the same height and their faces were now barely inches from each other. It wouldn't have surprised me if the confrontation had led to blows, but any possible escalation was averted by the arrival of a woman who came out through the French windows.

And not just any woman.

This lady was taller than either of the two men – probably taller than me – and she had shoulders like a bull. I reckoned she had to be in her sixties or even early seventies but she looked anything but frail. She certainly wasn't thin, but she wasn't obese by any means. Redoubtable, that was the word that came to mind, definitely redoubtable. She marched across to where the two men were still arguing and stepped in between them like a referee in a kids' boxing match.

'Thomas! Nikolaos! Stop it, both of you. Stop it this instant!'

It wouldn't have surprised me if she had picked them both up by the scruff of the neck and given them a good shaking. She was unmistakably English, dyed-in-the-wool old English, with the sort of accent that only a privileged family background and private education can produce. The man with the teacup looked relieved to see her, while his aggressor meekly released his hold, stepped away, and hung his head like a naughty schoolboy while the redoubtable lady addressed him in the stentorian tones of a stern headmistress.

'Nikolaos, you should be ashamed of yourself. You had every right to say what you said about Thomas's paper back in the hall, but you have absolutely no right to come out here and assault him.'

'He copied my work and sullied my reputation, trying to imply that my methods are unprofessional.' Greek, maybe? The accent reminded me of the very first holiday I had taken over there with my now ex-wife.

The hipster was quick to object. 'That's just plain wrong.' He turned towards the redoubtable lady. 'I would never do something like that, Violet, and I certainly wouldn't bother copying from somebody like Nick the Greek here.' Thomas was English, but without the patrician overtones of the lady standing alongside him. At a guess, Essex or somewhere around London, comprehensive school and a red brick university. His tone was sneeringly condescending and I found myself taking an instant dislike to him – not because of what I imagined to be his humble origins, not dissimilar to my own, but to his air of superiority. One of the reasons I never got promoted above DCI was that I have always had a bit of a problem with people who like to throw their weight around – like my old super, for example. And, after a diet of full

English breakfasts, fish and chips, and pints of Guinness, he had a lot of weight to throw around.

'What do you mean, somebody like me?' Nikolaos added something under his breath that quite plainly wasn't complimentary, but Violet was having none of it.

'Stop it, both of you. You're behaving like spoilt children. Nikolaos, if you believe Thomas copied or denigrated your work, you need to provide proof and publish it in the Journal. Thomas, I want you to keep away from Nikolaos for the rest of this symposium and the same applies to you, Nikolaos, or there will be consequences. Both of you keep well apart. Is that clear?' Sensing lingering resistance, she raised her voice. 'I said, is that clear?'

The custody sergeant at my old nick couldn't have done it better, and I saw both men nod in reluctant agreement. After an awkward silence, Thomas the Englishman swallowed the last of his tea – and there couldn't have been much of it left in the cup – turned on his heel and marched back inside. He was followed half a minute later by the lady I was already thinking of as the headmistress, leaving Nikolaos out there, obviously still fuming. I turned towards Anna and grinned.

'Professional rivalry. Tempers running high.'

She smiled back at me. She had been following the scene. 'He's an unhappy man but he's awfully good-looking, isn't he?'

'Who? Nikolaos or Thomas?'

'Nikolaos, of course.'

I took a better look at him. Up till now I hadn't considered assessing how physically appealing he might be, although his performance with the ladies at lunchtime would seem to confirm Anna's opinion. Grudgingly – this was my girlfriend talking, after all – I had to admit that she was right. 'I suppose so, if you like the slick, old nightclub crooner look.'

'Not so old. A lot younger than you...' She reached over and laid a reassuring hand on my arm. 'Much younger than both of us, *carissimo.*'

My attention was drawn back to the Greek as another figure appeared on the terrace and hurried across to him. I was fascinated to see that it was none other than Freja Blomqvist from Sweden, but this time she was no longer accompanied by the ginger-haired man. As further confirmation of Anna's opinion of the man and my designation of him as a Latin lover, he opened his arms to her and she wrapped herself affectionately around him and led him down into the garden and out of our sight. There was little doubt that Anna was right about Nikolaos appealing to the opposite sex. From my point of view, it was also a relief to see Freja clearly involved with another man. Hopefully, this would banish any lingering concerns Anna might have had about what might or might not have happened at the book signing.

* * *

That evening, Anna and I met up for dinner with Virgilio and Lina at eight and were shown to our table in the corner of the dining room by the door. Our table and those of a handful of other assorted private guests were separated from the symposium delegates by a series of huge, spiny cactus plants in terracotta pots that did a pretty good job of giving us a degree of privacy. The food here at the hotel was one of the main reasons Virgilio had chosen this place. We had met up with him and Lina just after midday, after our session with the Austrians, and had gone straight into lunch. This had consisted of a seafood risotto loaded with clams, mussels and prawns, followed by excellent braised beef in a mushroom and onion sauce that had tasted as good as it smelt.

Tonight, we started with mixed antipasti of bruschetta, some of the slices of unsalted bread topped with chopped tomatoes in thick olive oil and others topped with soft fresh goats' cheese and grilled aubergines. Along with this was a choice of different salami and freshly carved cured ham. We drank local red wine, which was excellent. This was followed by *crespelle al tartufo* – thin pancake wraps filled with spinach and ricotta and liberally flavoured with grated truffles. I knew by now not to fill up on starters as the main course was yet to come, but I could happily have cleared the whole dish set before us. I wondered idly how many kilos I was going to pack on over this brief holiday. Still, it would have been rude not to do justice to the chef's efforts, wouldn't it?

As we ate, we chatted. Virgilio and I had agreed in advance to do our best to limit our conversations this weekend to subjects other than policing – in deference to our long-suffering partners – and we were soon discussing the unexpected presence of wolves around us. Virgilio, not surprisingly, had already heard that they existed here in Tuscany. I queried with him whether the local wolfpacks presented a problem to farmers, particularly shepherds, and he confirmed my fears, but he did add an interesting codicil.

'You sometimes hear stories about lambs and poultry being taken, but interestingly, most of the farmers don't hate them as much as you would think. Apparently, the wolves are doing an increasingly good job of keeping down the deer and wild boar populations, which have been getting out of hand. Also, the farmers receive compensation for any livestock taken by wolves. Even so, a lot of them aren't happy about sharing the countryside with such savage animals but, when all's said and done, the wolves have as much right to be here as they have.'

I had already heard from my neighbours in the countryside near Florence about the damage that wild boars could do to crops, especially vineyards, where they often ripped whole rows of precious vines out of the ground with their powerful tusks, causing untold destruction. I glanced down at Oscar, who was sprawled at my feet pretending to sleep but keeping very close olfactory tabs on the food on the table above him.

'Well, just so long as the wolves don't try attacking my four-legged friend.'

'I wonder if Reiner and Suzy are troubled by wolves.' Anna was thinking back to that morning. At teatime, she had been telling Virgilio and Lina about the amazing fresco and bemoaning the fact that it was unlikely ever to be seen by anybody else. 'I could hear chickens when we were walking about. I hope none of them have been taken. It must be scary out there in the middle of nowhere. Can you imagine hearing wolves howling at the moon in the depths of the night? Give me somewhere a bit closer to civilisation any time.'

At that moment, we were interrupted by the sound of somebody tapping a microphone and the whine of feedback that made Oscar emit a little whine in sympathy. I peered through the spiny branches of a cactus and saw the headmistress figure, Violet, on her feet, making a presentation. This was to a shy-looking couple who were persuaded to get up out of their seats and go over to the top table to collect their award. From her performance outside on the terrace, I dare say Violet could probably have just bellowed her speech and managed without the microphone but now, amplified, her voice echoed around all four corners of what was a big dining room.

'And the Society's award for best individual research goes to Italo Gervasio and Carla Vespucci from the University of Turin for their fascinating work on the locomotive ability of gastropod molluscs.' There was a polite cheer from the symposium delegates followed by a round of applause before Violet held out her hands towards the winners. 'Many congratulations. Do tell us all about it.'

A serious-looking man with straggly, long, grey hair, not dissimilar in appearance to Einstein, went over to collect a certificate from her. Alongside him was a considerably younger woman. She was wearing a shapeless dress that did little to enhance her dumpy figure. Her black hair was tied back in a severe ponytail, while a pair of thick-rimmed, tortoiseshell glasses covered half her face. She looked even more reticent than her partner and she hung back so that Einstein could step up to the microphone. He cleared his throat before speaking in clear, if strongly accented, English.

'Colleagues, friends, thank you most sincerely for this honour, which I'm delighted to share with Carla, who has been an invaluable partner throughout.' He then launched into a highly technical discourse on the research that soon had me thoroughly bamboozled. As far as I could tell, gastropod molluscs in layman's language translated as slugs, and the couple's research had concentrated in particular on the consistency of the mucus the animals secreted and used when propelling themselves along the ground. I had just cleared my plate, but I noticed that the couple on the table further along from us were in the process of eating fresh oysters. The woman clearly understood at least the subject of the scientist's speech even if she, like the rest of us, probably got lost in the technical jargon, and I saw her set down the oyster shell she had been holding and leave it untouched on her plate. I didn't blame her. There's a limit to the amount of mucus one wants to hear about while eating, particularly when you are eating something that looks not dissimilar.

I deliberately returned the conversation on our table to something more appealing and queried with Anna and the others where they wanted to go over the following days. After a brief discussion, it was decided that we would head west to the old Abbey of San Galgano where, Anna told us, there was a sword stuck in a stone similar to the Arthurian legends. After that, according to Virgilio, we could go for lunch in a nearby hilltop town where the food was reputed to be excellent and the views over the Tuscan countryside equally satisfying. Then he had made reservations for lunch on Sunday at what he said was one of the best restaurants in Tuscany and it was bang in the centre of Siena. We would be able to enjoy a good meal and then walk around that historic city in the afternoon. As for Monday and Tuesday, we could decide what to do nearer the time. That all sounded great to me.

Fortunately, the prize-winning scientist had finished his discourse on slugs and mucus by the time our main course arrived. We had all opted for fish tonight and were presented with turbot in a lemon and ginger sauce, accompanied by roast fennel sprinkled with parmesan. It tasted as good as it looked and I was feeling pleasantly full by the end. Even so, I still managed to find room for panna cotta served with a blueberry and raspberry compote. We were on holiday, after all.

As we sat there at the end of the meal sipping our coffees, the delegates started leaving their tables and filing out past us. I spotted the ginger-haired wolf-faeces man chatting to Thomas, the Englishman who had been accused of plagiarism. This conversation, although I couldn't hear what they were saying, looked far more amicable than the one out on the terrace with the Greek scientist. Nikolaos, *Nick the Greek* as the Englishman had disparagingly called him, walked past, sandwiched between two completely different women and Anna and I exchanged glances. Evidently, this was one scientist whose interests extended beyond the confines of the laboratory. Freja followed a few minutes later, now looking even more alluring in a tight-fitting, little red dress, and was unsurprisingly surrounded by a gaggle of three or four random men, no doubt all vying for her favours. She must have noticed me through our barrier of cactus plants as she gave me a smile and a little wave. I smiled back as she and her coterie disappeared from the room.

This exchange of glances did not go unnoticed by my partner. 'I get the impression the poo lady likes you, Dan.' Anna nudged me in the ribs but gave me an indulgent look. 'Should I be feeling jealous? Don't forget, you're old enough to be her father.'

This was a bit of a stretch: my fifty-seventh birthday was coming up in two months' time and Freja had to be in her forties, but I didn't rise to the jibe. 'Considering my advanced years, I expect she was waving at Oscar, rather than me. Or maybe she was waving at you. You know, one academic appealing to another.'

She reached over and gripped my arm. 'I'm quite happy with my old policeman, thank you.'

'And I'm very happy with you, Professor. And it's *ex*-policeman, remember?'

'Once a cop, always a cop.'

I exchanged glances with Virgilio. We both knew she was right, but I couldn't help noticing the expression that flashed across Lina's face. For one horrible moment, I had a feeling I recognised it. I'd seen it, or something very similar to it, on my ex-wife's face enough times in the latter years of my unhappy marriage. I had always envied Virgilio his long-suffering wife who appeared to have accepted the fact that her husband was likely to be called away at all times of the day and night. Could it be that she was having second thoughts? Maybe Virgilio's idea of this last-minute long weekend away had been an attempt to mend a few bridges. Hopefully a few days without police business would do both Lina and Virgilio good. I really hoped so.

4

SATURDAY EARLY MORNING

I was woken at just after two o'clock in the morning by Oscar nudging my shoulder. This wasn't totally unexpected. Back home, he usually slept in his bed downstairs in the kitchen, so sharing a hotel bedroom with him for the first time had been a step into the unknown, not least as Anna was here as well. I opened my eyes and saw his head barely a few inches from my face, his eyes glowing green in the remarkably bright moonlight. Realising that he had my attention, he nudged me again with his nose and he was trying to climb onto the bed when I gently caught hold of his front paws and returned him to the floor. I pointed to his basket over by the window and addressed him in as assertive a manner as possible – no easy feat when whispering.

'No, Oscar, get off and go to bed. Your bed, got that? Now!'

Evidently, he must have got his possessive pronouns mixed up as he immediately tried to climb back onto *our* bed. Accepting the inevitable, I slipped out from underneath the lovely warm duvet and led him over to the window, where I indicated that he had to sleep in his basket. I glanced over my shoulder and saw that Anna was still horizontal and so hopefully sleeping, but I kept my voice down all the same.

'Now lie down and sleep. Down, Oscar, down.'

He finally got the message and subsided into his basket, but his eyes remained wide open. I squatted down beside him for a while to be sure he didn't get up and follow me back across the room and I stroked his ears – he likes that – until he finally appeared to drift off. At that point, I slowly stood up again and was about to tiptoe back to bed when a sound from outside startled me. It was unmistakably a howl; not a scream, a squawk, a squeal of tyres or a squeaky gate, it was definitely a howl – and we all know which animals howl at the moon. With the windows closed, it was hard to tell exactly, but it didn't sound as if the beast was very far away. I glanced down at Oscar but he was still sleeping. This was unexpected as I would have imagined that a dog would pick up on such a primal sound and for a moment, I wondered if this might just have been my imagination after our encounter with the wolf-poo couple this afternoon.

A second howl convinced me that I wasn't dreaming.

Leaving Oscar and Anna to their slumbers, I tiptoed over to the bathroom door and went inside, closing it behind me but not turning on the light. I went across to the window and opened it, feeling the crisp night air chill my bare torso as I did so. Staring out into the dark, I scanned the shadows of the garden carefully. The moon was almost full, which at least meant that I could clearly make out the shrubs, hedges and trees surrounding the hotel, but, disappointingly, there was no sign of a wolf. For a moment, I thought I saw a shape slip between the bushes and disappear around the side of the hotel, but it could just have been my imagination. Besides, what I thought I'd seen was too big to be a wolf or a dog and was more probably human than lupine, but who in their right mind would be out in the middle of the night when wolves were roaming about?

I must have stood there for almost ten minutes, getting steadily colder. The sound wasn't repeated so there seemed little point in risking catching my death Deciding that there was nothing more to be gained, I quietly closed the window again and returned to bed. Fortunately, neither of my companions in the room stirred and I was soon able to drift off to sleep.

Next morning dawned bright, clear and chilly, but the sparkling sunshine and the cloudless sky indicated that the temperature would soon climb back up again. After slipping out for a quick walk and a comfort break for Oscar, I returned to the room and told a somewhat sceptical Anna about the strange sounds in the night and asked if she had heard anything. She shook her head and confirmed what I already knew, namely that she had been fast asleep. When we got down for breakfast at eight o'clock, the first thing I did was query with Virgilio and Lina if they had heard anything in the night, but it appeared they had both been sleeping soundly. When I told them slightly sheepishly what I thought I'd heard, Virgilio's reaction was the same as Anna's had been and he gave me a quizzical look.

'You don't think the howling sound could have been the product of your imagination? After all, didn't you say that Oscar didn't react? I'm no expert, but I would have thought that even a domestic dog like this one could be expected to react to something as spooky as that.'

I nodded. 'I know what you mean, that's what I thought as well at first, but I'm pretty sure of what I heard. If it had just been the once then, yes, it could have been down to my subconscious, but by the time I heard that second howl, I'm quite sure I was wide awake.'

At that moment, our attention was attracted by a different

noise outside the window. This time it wasn't a wolf howling, but the all too familiar sound of the emergency services approaching at pace. Old habits die hard and Virgilio and I instinctively jumped to our feet and went across to the windows to peer out into the car park. Two police cars and an ambulance were lined up outside. As we looked on, a dark-blue Carabinieri Land Rover came tearing up the drive behind them and screeched to a halt, disgorging four uniformed officers, all carrying automatic weapons. I gave Virgilio a knowing look.

'Are you thinking what I'm thinking?'

He gave me a sceptical shake of the head. 'You must be joking. Didn't the dog-poo man say that there hasn't been a single wolf attack on a human for fifty years?'

'Well, maybe it wasn't an attack, but I bet it was wolves. Presumably somebody must have reported the presence of a pack near here – the ones I heard in the night – and the Carabinieri have been sent to get rid of them.'

Virgilio shook his head again. 'Not with guns. Wolves are a protected species nowadays. Besides, if it was just a bit of vermin clearance, it's unlikely that so many units would have responded. And why an ambulance? No, it's pretty clear something's happened, but I bet you a bottle of Chianti that it had nothing to do with wolves.'

I'm sure it came as no surprise to either of our partners when he and I excused ourselves and went out to see what was going on. I couldn't help checking Lina's face as Virgilio announced his intentions. For a second or two, I'm sure I saw the same haunted expression I had noticed the previous night and I almost called him back, but the moment passed and Lina's normal, peaceful expression returned. I murmured a silent prayer that all was well between the two of them. Being married to a police officer could take a toll on relationships, as I knew to my cost.

Until we knew better what was happening, I left Oscar in Anna's care just to be on the safe side and followed Virgilio out into the car park. The first face we saw when we stepped out of the front door turned out to be familiar to Virgilio, who gave him a cheerful welcome.

'*Ciao*, Bruno, it's good to see you again.'

The two men shook hands.

'Well, well, well, Virgilio, fancy meeting you here. Are you on duty or is this a social visit?' Bruno was probably ten years younger than me and was wearing a leather jacket and jeans. His accent was Tuscan.

Virgilio shook his head. 'Definitely not work. Lina and I are here on holiday for a few days with Dan and his partner. Let me introduce you. This is Dan Armstrong, formerly Chief Inspector Armstrong of the murder squad in London. Dan, this is Detective Inspector Bruno Senese from the *squadra mobile* in Siena. He makes the best *zuccotto* this side of Florence.' He grinned. 'And Bruno's a great detective as well as an amazing cook.'

I shook the inspector's hand and was surprised to find that my fame had preceded me.

'*Commisario* Armstrong, I've heard about you. You're a private investigator now, aren't you? Weren't you the person who managed to locate the runaway daughter of Contessa Delmare?'

I nodded. I remembered the countess and her daughter well. The seventeen-year-old had got into bad company and it had been by sheer chance that I had spotted her while I was keeping tabs on a Florentine man whose wife suspected him of dabbling in drugs. Fortunately, I had recognised the girl's face from a missing persons bulletin and so was able to reunite her with her mother, who immediately sent her off to a detox clinic. The girl hadn't appeared any too pleased to see her mother, and I had often wondered since then what had happened to her.

'Good to meet you, Bruno, and it's just Dan these days. What brings you and your colleagues out in force here today?'

His face assumed a more serious expression. 'You're not going to believe this, but it looks as though we've just had the first wolf attack in Italy for God knows how many decades.'

Virgilio and I exchanged glances and he took over the questioning. 'A serious attack? Was anybody badly hurt?'

'One man: mauled, mutilated and killed, I'm afraid.' He turned to a uniformed officer who had been standing patiently alongside him. 'Where's the body?'

'This way, sir.' The young officer pointed off to the right, towards the rear of the building. 'The hotel gardener found the body early this morning and called 112. My sergeant and I were the first to arrive. The sergeant's still there now, keeping watch so that nobody can interfere with it. We've cordoned off the area, waiting for you to come.'

Bruno and Virgilio nodded approvingly and I suddenly realised that I was doing the exact same thing. What was that about old habits? It was good to see that these officers were doing things by the book.

'Excellent, well, let's go and take a look.' Bruno looked across at Virgilio. 'You're welcome to come along, but don't let me keep you from the ladies.'

'Are you kidding? A wolf attack? I can't miss this.' Virgilio shot me a glance. 'What about you, Dan?'

'I feel the same way – not a lot of wolf attacks in London – but I promised Anna this weekend would be all about her. Thanks, but I'd better leave you to it.' Having already allowed the commitments of my former job to screw up my marriage, the last thing I wanted was to screw up this new relationship with Anna. Besides, I reminded myself, it wasn't as if I were still in the force so it was no longer my job. Remembering the looks on his wife's face, I very nearly suggested to Virgilio to follow my example, but I chickened out at the last minute. Getting involved with a friend's marital problems can open a can of worms.

The uniformed officer clearly felt he should prepare the other two for the sight that awaited them. 'I'm afraid it's not pretty, sir. The animals have made a real mess of the guy.'

From the look on Virgilio's face when he returned to the breakfast table five minutes later, the officer hadn't been exaggerating. Even with all his years of experience of violent death, Virgilio was looking appalled. His wife must have recognised that look and I saw her reach over to catch hold of his hand.

'It's happened, Virgilio, and there's nothing you can do about it. Let the local police deal with it. Remember, this is meant to be a holiday.'

He gave her a weary smile and nodded. 'Yes, of course. Besides, an animal attack is hardly the business of the murder squad.'

'So was it really a wolf?' I could hardly believe my ears. I gave him a little smile and tried to cheer him up. 'So that's a bottle of Chianti you owe me.'

'That's what it looks like, but Bruno's going to wait until he gets the verdict of Forensics. I'm not convinced so the bet's still on for now. The pathology team have just arrived.'

We were finishing breakfast when the same young police officer appeared and came across to speak to Virgilio. 'The inspector asks if you could spare him a moment, sir. The pathologist has found something interesting and the inspector would welcome your opinion.'

Virgilio stood up and glanced across at me. 'You coming, Dan?'

Interested as I was – not at the idea of blood and gore, but at the possibility of the attack having been carried out by the animal I had heard in the night – I still shook my head, hoping Virgilio would take the hint and do the same. 'No, you go if you like, but remember, you're on holiday. I promised Anna...'

I felt Anna's hand on my arm. 'It's all right, Dan. Oscar's been telling me he'd like another walk so why don't you go along with Virgilio, while Lina and I take Oscar to see if he can find any squirrels to chase?'

'Are you sure?'

She leant over and gave me a peck on the cheek. 'Go. I know you're dying to and I don't mind. Honestly.'

I kissed her in return but without having the nerve to check Lina's face to see how she might be reacting to the idea.

5

SATURDAY MORNING

I followed Virgilio and the young police officer outside. When we turned the corner of the building and saw the taped-off area, it was clear that the attack had taken place almost directly in front of the window of our room among the meticulously pruned rosemary bushes. This appeared to confirm that the howls I had heard had indeed been produced by the animal responsible for the attack.

Somebody had covered the body with a sheet, and the pathologist was standing to one side, deep in conversation with the inspector. They looked up as we approached and Bruno indicated the pathologist. 'Donatella here has made a discovery. See what you gentlemen think.'

The pathologist crouched down and lifted a corner of the sheet with her gloved hand. The body was lying face down and she had shaved a patch in the thick, dark hair on the back of his skull. Virgilio and I leant forward to take a closer look and it was immediately apparent that there was a hefty red and blue bruise there that had discoloured the skin and drawn a few drops of blood.

'Could a wolf or a dog have done that?' Virgilio asked the question that was on my lips and we both saw the pathologist shake her head.

'Impossible. That bruise was inflicted with a blunt instrument, not fangs or claws.'

'Could he have fallen onto something hard?'

'We've done a search all around here and it's just grass and soft earth. No stones, no bricks, nothing metal. I suppose it's possible he fell and hit his head elsewhere and was crawling back when he was set upon by a pack of wolves. We're doing a search but so far no signs of that.'

'So would the blow to the head have killed him?'

Once again, the pathologist shook her head. 'The cause of death was almost certainly exsanguination – I'll know better once I've done a full post-mortem – but a blow powerful enough to do this much damage to his skull would almost certainly have rendered the victim unconscious for a while and very woolly when he woke up – if he woke up.'

Virgilio and I straightened up and looked across at the inspector, who nodded grimly. 'So it looks as though we may have a murder on our hands after all.'

I looked back down at the pathologist, who was still crouched beside the shrouded figure of the victim. 'If he bled to death, what was responsible for all the loss of blood? Was he really attacked by wolves, maybe after he was knocked out?'

The pathologist pulled back the sheet, reached forward and rolled the body over. I was immediately struck not so much by the horrific injuries to the victim's throat, neck and chest but by the fact that I recognised his face.

'I know this guy. I saw him yesterday. He's one of the delegates in the ecological symposium. I don't know his surname but his first name is Nikolaos. He's Greek.'

'Doctor Nikolaos Diamantis.' The pathologist picked up a plastic card attached to a bloodstained lanyard and dangled it before us. 'This was in his pocket.'

'Poor guy.' I looked back down at the battered remains of the man Anna had described as very good-looking and I had christened Casanova and shook my head slowly. 'Well, I'm afraid he won't be charming any more ladies.'

'Do you think these wounds were inflicted by wolves?' Virgilio was still sounding sceptical and, now that there was a possibility that it had been murder, I knew I had to be equally cautious about jumping to conclusions. My bottle of Chianti was looking less certain by the minute.

'Again, I'll know more after the autopsy.' The pathologist glanced at her watch. 'I should be able to tell you something more definite this afternoon but, for now, ignoring the blow to the head, I suppose it's possible these slashes and rips could be the work of a big carnivore.'

'Or of somebody trying to make it look as though they'd been made by a big carnivore.' I was just thinking out loud, but I saw both detectives and the pathologist nod in agreement.

Bruno thanked the pathologist and told her she and her team could remove the body. He then instructed the four uniformed officers to conduct a minute search of the nearby area. 'In particular, see if you can find whatever it was that hit him on the head and check all the soft ground to see if there are any paw or footprints. There are no traces here on the grass, but you should be able to pick up the trail when you get to the flower borders at the edges of the lawn. I'll give orders that this area of the gardens is out of bounds for now.'

We walked back in the direction of the hotel and stopped by an ornamental fountain where chubby cherubs frolicked with a pair of dolphins spouting water from their mouths. It was a charming, peaceful scene and it seemed barely credible that a violent assault had taken place only a few metres away.

The inspector was looking pensive. 'Until we know for sure whether we're looking for an animal or a human, we'd better keep an open mind and work on the basis that it could be murder. I'll give instructions that nobody's to leave the premises. I understand that the hotel's full because there's some sort of conference going on. How many of the attendees are likely to speak Italian?'

Virgilio and I shook our heads in unison and he answered for both of us. 'Not very many, I would think. The *lingua franca* of the symposium is pretty clearly English.'

Now it was Bruno's turn to shake his head. 'That's a complication I could have done without. If Donatella confirms foul play, we're going to have to take statements from everybody in the hotel, and language is going to be a real problem. My English is monosyllabic and the officers in my department aren't much better.' He stopped and caught my eye. I had a feeling I knew what was coming next – and I was right. 'You speak great Italian, Dan. I don't suppose you feel like making yourself some pocket money, do you? I'll see you get top rate.'

If I had received this request on any other weekend I would have agreed immediately, but this time I hesitated. 'I'd better check with Anna first. Can you give me a couple of minutes?'

'Of course. But it would be a big help if you could... even just for a few hours until we can sort out an official interpreter.'

I went back up to our room but it was empty so I headed outside to see if I could find Anna and Oscar. As I hurried along the *strada bianca* through the vines, I heard running footsteps and a figure appeared around the corner coming towards me. It was Freja Blomqvist, aka Uncle Jack, out for a run in a pair of spandex shorts and a crop top. She slowed to a halt as she reached me and gave me the sort of warm smile that would have had stronger-willed men than me falling at her feet. Fortunately, I was already in a meaningful relationship – and, besides, as my girlfriend had reminded me none too subtly, I was a lot older than the blonde bombshell and would do well to remember that.

She trained those amazing light-blue eyes on me. 'Good morning, Dan. Have you any idea what's going on at the hotel with all the police cars?'

It occurred to me that it could be useful to get the opinion of a wolf expert. 'I'm afraid somebody's been killed. From the look of it, it might have been a wolf attack.'

A range of different expressions flitted across her face, ranging from horror to incredulity, but, call me suspicious if you like, maybe she didn't look as surprised as all that. 'That's ridiculous. Didn't Pavel tell you yesterday how little we have to fear from wolves? Who's been killed?'

Remembering the way she had cosied up to the Greek the previous afternoon, I took refuge in obfuscation. 'I don't know, I'm afraid, but I heard that the police pathologist is still trying to establish cause of death.'

'Well, it's definitely not wolves, I can assure you of that.' There could be no doubting the conviction in her tone. 'They never attack humans.'

'What about if they found a dead human? Would they eat the body?'

'Only if they were desperately hungry, and for wolves around here there's plenty of game to eat, not to mention farms with poultry and new lambs in the fields. Wolves know our scent, you see, and they would normally stay well clear of anything that smells human. Why, had something been eating the body?'

Thinking back on it, although the victim had been badly mutilated, I didn't remember any missing bits. From what Freja was saying, the chances of a wolf attack appeared even slimmer and, in consequence, it was looking ever more likely that we had a murder on our hands. I gave her a non-committal shrug. 'Sorry, I don't know. I was just wondering.'

While she set off at a run back in the direction of the hotel, I carried on up the path. Before too long, she was going to learn the identity of the victim, and I had a feeling it was going to come as a very unwelcome surprise to her – or at least it should do. But I still couldn't shift that feeling that she hadn't been completely surprised to hear about the death.

A couple of hundred yards further on, I caught up with Anna and Lina accompanied by Oscar. As the Labrador jumped up to greet me, Anna caught hold of my arm just as Lina had done to Virgilio.

'Was it horrid?'

I nodded. 'Pretty grim but guess who the victim is... Nick the Greek.'

Her face fell. 'How awful. What a terrible shame.'

I chose to assume that her sympathetic reaction was purely at the death of a fellow human being, rather than at the tragic loss to womankind of a particularly desirable male. I told her how it was looking possible and ever more likely that it had in fact been murder, and she gasped in surprise.

'Who would want to kill a simple scientist? As far as I know, the symposium's all about conservation and ecology; both vitally important to the future of the planet, but hardly the sort of thing that excites international spy agencies or people like that. It's not as if he was dealing in nuclear secrets or ballistic missiles. Do they think it was somebody here at the hotel who did it?'

I had been asking myself the same question. 'I honestly don't know. We saw him having that argument with the English guy yesterday but that looked more like handbags at dawn than anything more sinister. As for the others, I don't know them, but if it *is* murder, the inspector from the Siena murder squad has asked for my help with interpreting. He'll have to interview everybody in the hotel, you see.' I averted my eyes and kept them on Oscar, who was fully occupied scratching his ear with his hind leg. 'Would you mind if I lent a hand? I know I promised to try and make this a weekend without business, but this is a bit exceptional, after all...'

'Of course I don't mind, you idiot. If somebody's been murdered, it's the duty of all of us to help. Presumably this means our trip down to San Galgano is off?'

'From what the inspector said, he wants everybody to stay on the premises or at least close by, so I suppose we're stuck here for the rest of the day. Are you sure you don't mind?'

'Of course I don't mind; we can do it on Monday or some other time. Besides, I'll have Lina and Oscar to keep me company.' She paused for thought. 'Come to think of it, if they're stuck for people to help interpret, I could also offer my services, couldn't I?'

I grinned back at her. 'The inspector said we'd get paid for our time so, you never know, we might end up making a profit on the weekend.'

6

SATURDAY LUNCHTIME

The call from the pathologist came through just after two while we were drinking our coffees after another excellent meal – this time an open buffet with everything from crayfish and prawns to the best Caesar salad I had ever eaten. Inspector Bruno had joined us for lunch and it came as no surprise to note that the atmosphere in the rest of the dining room was strained. Although I had overheard a few participants sounding indignant that they were being forced to stay in the hotel or its grounds for now, most people just appeared shell-shocked. From what I'd been able to understand, the symposium sessions had been cancelled this morning, but when people started getting up at the end of lunch and filing out, I heard them talking about returning to the conference centre where things were due to pick up again.

Among the faces I recognised was Violet, the headmistress figure, who was looking unexpectedly distraught. I had evidently been doing her an injustice as I had somehow imagined her reaction would have been more one of annoyance that the symposium was being interrupted than of pity for the dead man, but her eyes were red and her manner crushed. Clearly, deep down she wasn't as crusty as her redoubtable exterior would suggest.

There was no sign of Freja, which wasn't surprising if she had been a close friend of the victim. She was quite likely in her room crying at this very moment. Thomas, the supercilious Englishman, looked unmoved but I already knew that there had been no love lost between him and the Greek. I studied his features carefully as he walked past but I couldn't immediately see any signs of culpability. He had just gone out through the door when I felt a tap on my shoulder. It was Freja's ginger-haired wolf-poo friend from yesterday. He was looking anxious – whether this was out of fear remained to be seen and, if so, fear of what or whom?

'I was speaking to Freja earlier and she told me the police think it was a wolf attack. Is that really what they think? Surely not?'

I pointed across the table towards Bruno. 'This is Inspector Senese from the Siena murder squad who's come to investigate, and this is my friend Inspector Pisano from Florence. What's your name, please?'

He held out his ID card. 'Havel... Doctor Pavel Havel. I'm from Charles University in Prague, but it can't be wolves...' Just like Freja, he sounded appalled at the thought and I tried to pacify him.

'Nobody knows for sure at the moment, but there's an autopsy going on as we speak.' While I rattled off a quick translation to Bruno, Virgilio answered the scientist in his pretty good English.

'We understand that a number of participants here are experts on wolves. Presumably that includes you?'

Pavel Havel nodded. 'There are two of us here who specialise in large carnivores, principally bears and wolves. There's Freja from Stockholm University and I'm based in Prague, but the two of us share the same area of research. So I suppose you can say we're experts.'

'Did you say bears? Are there bears in Italy?' Anna looked up from her coffee with interest.

'Yes, but not around here. There are a few dozen brown bears in parts of the Alps and further south in Lazio and Abruzzo, quite a long way from where we are now, but their numbers are still very limited.'

'Aren't they considered dangerous?'

He shook his head. 'Not really. Like with wolves, there are always some people who think large carnivores should be exterminated. Those people tend to be more from the agricultural community, but most other people adopt a live-and-let-live policy.'

Virgilio continued. 'I see, and do you know if Doctor Diamantis was involved in any specific research? Anything contentious?'

'Not that I know of. He was a marine biologist, specialising in marine fissipeds.' Seeing the expressions on our faces, he elaborated. 'Marine mammals like polar bears and sea otters, I believe, but, although they're linked to my field of interest, I had no dealings with him.'

'And your other colleagues here, what are their fields of interest?'

'A broad spectrum. We're all concerned with conservation and there are experts here in all kinds of flora and fauna from around the world. We have delegates here not only from Europe but also from Asia and Africa as well as America, north and south.'

'What about the lady in charge of the symposium?'

'Professor Grosvenor, she's the president of our society. Her area's principally cetaceans and sirenians.' He had to explain again for our benefit. 'She's also a sea mammal specialist but in her case it's whales, porpoises, manatees and so on.' An expression of apprehension appeared on his face. 'Why are you asking all these questions? Do you think Nikolaos might have been murdered by somebody here?' His eyes were just about bulging out of his head.

Virgilio adopted a soothing tone. 'Not necessarily, we just wanted to get a bit of background. Inspector Senese here is keeping an open mind for now while he and his people continue with their enquiries. It may turn out to be murder or it might prove to be animal attack.'

Doctor Havel appeared to have little doubt. 'It has to be murder. Like I keep saying, this tragic death can't be the work of wolves; they don't attack humans. Please, whatever you do, don't start saying that, or you could set back the cause of conservation by years and years. There's a lot of folklore about wolves and it wouldn't need much to turn the population against them. They were almost hunted to extinction only a few decades ago and if their protected species status were to be reversed, it could be catastrophic, not just for the wolves, but for the whole ecosystem around here.'

It was plain to see that he was passionate about his subject and I could understand his concern. It appeared that Bruno felt the same way, but he didn't mince his words when he replied, and I translated for the scientist's benefit. 'Until we get confirmation one way or another from the pathology lab, all options are on the table. However, if it turns out that wolves were responsible, I'm afraid I'll have no choice but to inform the appropriate authorities. What happens after that will be out of my hands... Excuse me, this is the pathologist.'

He picked up his phone that had started vibrating on the tabletop and answered tersely, just giving his name, 'Senese.'

Doctor Havel hovered nervously by the table while Bruno spoke on the phone. After a couple of minutes, the call ended and the inspector looked up at the scientist. I translated as he relayed the content of the call. 'The good news, Doctor Havel, as far as you're concerned, is that we are now definitely dealing with a murder. Whoever killed your colleague walks on two legs, not four, even if he or she tried to make it look as though an animal was to blame.'

A wave of relief washed across the scientist's face. 'Thank you, Inspector, that's the best possible news I could have received.'

He was already turning away to pass on the good news to his fellow conservationists when Virgilio added the obvious corollary to this. 'It depends whether you consider the very real possibility that we have a murderer in our midst as good news or bad. Personally, it makes me feel uncomfortable.'

The other man's face fell as realisation dawned. 'Yes, yes, of course. I wasn't thinking.'

Virgilio then asked him the question that I knew we were going to be asking a lot in the course of the next few hours. 'Tell me, have you any idea who might have killed Doctor Diamantis?'

The other man shook his head. 'Ever since I heard about his death, I've been wondering the same thing. I honestly don't know anybody here who had the sort of grudge against him that could lead to murder. Maybe somebody in Geneva?'

'That's where he was living?'

'Either in the city or somewhere close by. He works... worked at Geneva University. He spoke excellent French as well as English.'

'Thank you, Doctor Havel.' After the other man went off, Bruno relayed the full content of the call from the pathologist.

'Time of death between one and four this morning. Donatella says that the victim did indeed die of exsanguination but that he was almost certainly already unconscious when the fatal wounds were inflicted as there are no signs that he attempted to defend himself. The slashes and cuts across his throat and torso that killed him were made with a broken bottle or something similar presumably so as to give the impression of it having been done by a wolf. Donatella's located a couple of particles of broken glass in the wounds, which would seem to confirm that. As far as I'm concerned, trying to blame it on a wolf when all these scientists know that they wouldn't kill humans makes it less likely to me that the killer is one of the people here. It strikes me that it has to be somebody less knowledgeable, maybe somebody completely divorced from the symposium.'

I felt I had to point out the problem with that assumption. 'You may well be right, but I doubt whether everybody at this symposium really does know that wolves don't attack humans. Would a specialist in, say, orchids or stick insects, know much about carnivores? Maybe there's an argument for this charade having been put on by one of the symposium attendees, but just somebody with much less knowledge of the subject.' I hesitated as something else occurred to me. My ex-wife often accused me of never being able to take anything at face value and I could almost hear her voice mocking me as I continued. 'Alternatively, maybe it was done by somebody at the symposium who knew full well that it couldn't have been a wolf, but who did it so as to make it look as though it wasn't done by a carnivore specialist.'

I saw this idea register with Bruno and he gave me a wry smile. 'You've got an even more warped brain than I have, Dan. Have you ever thought about joining the police?'

I smiled back. 'Been there, done that and happily retired, thanks.'

Virgilio snorted. 'Retired? You must be joking. He never stops, does he, Anna?'

I turned towards her in alarm. This was a bit of a sore point between us as I struggled to build up my new investigative business and tried to cultivate the relatively new relationship with

Anna at the same time. She gave me a placating smile before answering Virgilio.

'I know, but that's just the way he's made. I went into this relationship with my eyes open, so I can't complain.'

While Anna was speaking, I glanced across at Lina. I couldn't miss the slight narrowing of her eyes and the tightening of her lips and my heart sank. Even if I had been blind to these same signs for years in my own marriage, I now knew and recognised them all too well. I had a horrible feeling that Virgilio's job might finally be impacting their marriage and I felt a wave of sympathy for both of them.

Meanwhile, Bruno had been thinking. 'Well, there's nothing for it; we need to interview everybody here at the hotel: scientists, ordinary guests and all the members of staff. From what I've been told, that means somewhere between ninety and a hundred people. I've already got a team doing a sweep of the area where the body was found but I'll get them to check out any neighbouring properties. It seems unlikely that any of the locals would even know a Greek professor from Switzerland, but we need to be sure one way or another.'

I nodded approvingly and glanced across at Anna. 'That will probably include our friends Reiner and Suzy. Who knows? With his dislike of scientists, maybe he rode over on the horse to commit the murder?' Seeing the immediate interest on Bruno's face, I was quick to explain that I was joking – or at least I thought I was – but I couldn't help reflecting that Reiner was a weird sort of character, maybe even a sociopath, and I had met enough sociopaths who had killed in my time. Surely not?

In the meantime, Bruno had a question for Anna. 'As somebody from the world of academia rather than law enforcement, what's your gut feeling? Could he have been murdered by one of the other scientists here? Do you think professional jealousy could get so out of hand that it resulted in murder?'

She shook her head. 'I would think that highly unlikely, in fact, virtually impossible. My instinct, and that's all it is, is that I have a feeling there may be a woman in the mix. He was a *very* good-looking man, after all.'

Virgilio told Bruno about Nikolaos Diamantis's flirting with a variety of women at lunch the previous day as well as the scene we had witnessed on the terrace that afternoon, up to and including the affectionate way Freja the Swede had wrapped herself around him. I added my hunch that she maybe hadn't been as surprised as all that to hear that there had been a death. Anna then further dented my self-esteem by giving a rapturous description of the Greek's appearance and his obvious appeal to members of the opposite – or indeed his own – sex. Clearly, we needed to establish what relationship there might have been between him and Freja but, considering that she lived in northern Europe while he had lived two thousand kilometres away from her in Switzerland, it seemed unlikely that this could have been a relationship of any great depth.

Bruno nodded. 'You may well be right. Sex and money are still two of the prime motivators when it comes to murder, although jealousy – either professional or emotional – can play its part as well. One thing's for sure, there's no longer any question of blaming it on wolves.'

Virgilio looked across at me and smiled. 'So I believe you owe me a bottle of Chianti.'

I nodded. 'So it would seem. Pity we're no longer in the Chianti region.'

His smile broadened. 'Good try, but that's where you're wrong. We're right at the southern end of the Chianti area now but still inside it. We're in the Colli Senesi and it just so happens there's a very good producer only a few hundred metres away from where we are now.'

I grinned back. 'All right, I admit defeat. The wolves are in the clear and you'll get your bottle.'

'Excellent.' Suddenly more serious, he glanced over at Anna. 'Please don't think us heartless for joking about trivia so soon after the death of a man, but I suppose it's a sort of defence mechanism. That's the problem with being in the police. It can be difficult to switch off.'

I saw his wife reach over to squeeze his hand as Anna replied. 'I can imagine, Virgilio, and I know you both well enough by now.' She then adopted a businesslike air and turned towards Bruno. 'So, what would you like us to do this afternoon?'

Before he could answer, Virgilio chimed in. 'Bruno, as you've got a lot of people to deal with, I'm happy to do some of the interviews if it helps out.'

Even if I hadn't already had my suspicions, the look that spread across Lina's face as she listened to her husband's offer was all too easy to read and I very nearly said something, but in the end I bit my tongue and decided it wasn't my battle to fight. At least, not yet.

Apparently unaware of the tension in the air, the inspector nodded gratefully. 'That's very kind, Virgilio. So, seeing as I'm in the fortunate position of having *two* experienced detective inspectors here with me, I'll divide the interviewees into four groups. Anna, why don't you interpret for me with my interviews while Virgilio and Dan deal with the other English speakers? I'll give you one of my officers each for support. My men can handle all the Italian speakers. Okay?'

Virgilio turned towards Lina with a smile. 'You don't mind if I help out, do you, *carissima*? You can have a lazy afternoon in the spa, can't you?'

There was no answering smile, but she nodded her head. 'Of course, you've got to do what you've got to do.'

This time, Anna must have heard it as well, because I felt her grip my hand under the table and give my fingers a squeeze. Virgilio, whose investigative skills and deductive powers were normally admirable, gave his wife a little peck on the cheek and stood up, rubbing his palms together happily.

'Great, can't wait to get started.'

The pressure on my fingers increased and I could tell that Anna felt I should say something, but what? This wasn't the time or the place to get involved with somebody else's marital problems. But I had a sinking feeling that that time was fast approaching.

7

SATURDAY AFTERNOON

The interviews took up most of the afternoon. Bruno divided up the names and I sat down in a side room with Oscar at my feet and alongside me the young police officer who had been the first on the scene. He told me his name was Constable Gori and he and I had the chance to chat as we worked our way through the interviews, recording the replies and making notes as we went along. It emerged that this was only his first year in the force and the very first time he had witnessed such a badly mutilated murder victim. He was holding up well, but I could see that it had hit him hard and I did my best to encourage him. I remembered my first experience of something like this: a corpse dragged out of the Thames after being found submerged in the water. I could imagine what he was going through. I was delighted to discover that his English was better than I had expected and he managed to take notes without my having to translate every single word.

Either by accident or by design, I didn't have Freja Blomqvist in my group, but I did have the headmistress. Professor Violet Grosvenor of Cambridge University was looking and sounding a lot less redoubtable now, but murder can do that to a person. I took it slowly as I worked through the list of questions that Bruno, Virgilio and I had agreed between us. As she was the current president of the conservation society, I started by asking about the symposium itself and discovered that this was an annual event, being held in Italy for only the first time. I queried why they had chosen this location and the answer came as a bit of a surprise.

'It was mainly because of the marquis.' Before I could ask, she explained. 'The Marquis of San Bartolomeo has long been a patron of our society and he's extended a standing invitation to our members for some years now to visit his lovely home.'

'And that is where? Surely he doesn't own the hotel.'

'In fact he does, but this isn't his home. He lives in the Castel San Bartolomeo, which is only about five minutes to the south of us by car. All the delegates are invited there for a farewell dinner on Tuesday night. Do you think we'll be allowed to go, or will we still be confined to the hotel?'

That was three days away and I hoped the investigation might be wrapped up by then, but I kept it vague. 'I don't really know. It depends on what progress the inspector makes with the investigation. I'll make sure he knows about this, though, and I would hope it'll be possible.' I glanced over at Gori to check that he had made a note of this and saw him nod before I continued. 'How are you planning on getting there?'

'We have two coaches booked to pick us up from here at 7 p.m. on Tuesday and return us to the hotel at midnight. There was going to be dancing but, after what's happened, I'm sure it'll be a much more subdued affair.'

'I'll tell the inspector. Now, just for the record – we're asking everybody this – please can you confirm where you were between the end of dinner last night and breakfast today?'

If she was affronted to be asked to provide details of her movements, she didn't show it. 'Immediately after dinner, I went through to the conference centre for a meeting with the other committee members to finalise the programme for the next three days.'

'How long has the symposium been running?'

'It's a five-day event, Friday to Tuesday inclusive, but of course today has been seriously disrupted. Normally Sunday is a free day and we have an excursion to Siena planned, if that's going to be allowed to go ahead. After today's tragedy, we're going to have to reschedule the programme so as to fit in the sessions that we've missed today, most probably by reducing tomorrow's Siena excursion to half a day and working tomorrow morning to catch up. We've just been talking over lunch, but there's no way we can extend things into Wednesday because people have flights booked and commitments elsewhere to honour.'

'Can you give me the names of the committee members, please?'

'There are just four committee members, plus me.' She went on to list the names of three men and one woman and these were duly recorded before I moved the interview along.

'And how long did the meeting last?'

'About an hour. I can remember that it was almost ten-thirty when I got back to my room. After that I went to bed and didn't emerge until breakfast at seven-thirty and then, of course, there was the awful news about Nikolaos.'

'Is there anybody who can confirm you never left your room?'

She gave me a frosty look. 'I was alone. No, nobody can vouch for me, but I assure you I did *not* leave my room.'

'Thank you. And did you know the victim well?'

'Reasonably well. I've met him a few times at events like this, but never on a one-to-one basis.'

'Was there anybody here with whom he was particularly close?'

Maybe there was something in my tone but she glanced up sharply and there might even have been a glimmer of amusement in her eyes. 'I imagine you've been listening to some of the stories about Nikolaos, haven't you?'

I had a feeling I knew what she was talking about but pleaded ignorance. 'And what sort of stories might those be?'

'Let's just say that he had a bit of a reputation with the ladies.' I was mildly surprised not to hear disapproval in her voice. She could have been talking about a particularly frisky puppy.

'Any of the ladies here this weekend?'

As if regretting her moment of levity, she morphed back into her more forbidding, authority-figure persona. 'How other people spend their free time is no concern of mine. If Nikolaos was involved in any liaisons with any of the other symposium attendees, it was not brought to my attention.'

'I appreciate your discretion, Professor, but this is a murder investigation. Are you sure you can't give me any names?'

There was a brief pause while she was clearly making up her mind whether to descend to my level or not before she reluctantly relented. 'I suggest you have a talk to Marie-France – she would know better than I about that sort of thing.'

'That's Marie-France...?'

'Professor Marie-France Pelletier, formerly of the biology department at Lyon University.'

I let my eyes skim down over the list of attendees I had to interview this afternoon and was pleased to see the French professor's name on there. 'Do you think this lady might have had a romantic involvement with the victim?'

That same glimmer of amusement flashed momentarily across the august lady's face. 'I think that unlikely but, like I say, Marie-France has always kept her ear to the ground and I'm sure she'll know more than I do.'

And now I pitched her the hundred-thousand-dollar question. 'Can you think of anybody who might have committed this crime? Anybody with a grudge against Doctor Diamantis? Maybe the Englishman he had a spat with on the terrace yesterday afternoon in which you had to intervene?'

'Thomas? Hardly. I know there have been allegations aimed at Thomas – by Nikolaos and a number of others – about some questionable professional practices and about his scornful attitude to some other scientists, but there's no way he could be a murderer. At a guess, I would think he would faint at the sight of blood. As for anybody else, particularly any of our colleagues here at this symposium, I would be amazed if any of them were involved.'

'And Nikolaos wasn't working on anything secret, anything that might have made him the target for some shadowy government agency?' I was clutching at straws and she was bright enough to realise.

'Absolutely not, unless you buy into the tales of Russian polar bears wearing cameras or sea otters carrying mines.'

'Do such things exist?'

She snorted. 'Of course they don't. Some people have too much imagination; that's just science fiction. No, I really can't think of any reason anybody might have had for killing poor Nikolaos.' She then went on to say pretty much what Anna had said. 'Of course, he was a *very* handsome man, so maybe jealousy or unrequited love might be a motive, but I would hardly expect to find somebody prepared to stoop to murder among such a group of eminent scientists.'

* * *

In the course of the afternoon, Gori and I worked our way through the other potential witnesses but with no appreciable results until we came to the French scientist from Lyon University. When Professor Pelletier walked in, I started to realise why my suggestion that she might have been romantically involved with the victim had sparked that glimmer of amusement on the face of Professor Grosvenor. I've never been great at estimating the ages of older ladies, but this one had to be well over eighty, even if she was dressed in jeans, bright-yellow trainers and a red sweatshirt with Che Guevara's face on it. I was surprised I hadn't noticed her before as she would definitely stand out in a crowd. Even Oscar looked up and did a double take. Professor Pelletier had an unruly mass of spiky, white hair that spread out from her head in all directions, making her look like a cross between the blond one of the Marx Brothers and Medusa. There was what looked like a tattoo on the back of one of her hands, huge earrings the size of doughnuts hanging halfway down the sides of her head, and bracelets jingling on her thin, little wrists. Gori instinctively stood up and offered her a seat and she smiled at him.

'Thank you, young man.' She leant her walking stick against the arm of the chair and sat down opposite me. 'Now, how can I help?' If I hadn't been told she was French, I would have had her pegged for a member of the English upper classes. Her English was impeccable and her accent was even fruitier then Violet Grosvenor's. Her hands were racked with arthritis but her green eyes were still bright and there was a friendly expression on her wrinkled face. I took an immediate liking to her and it appeared that the same could be said for my dog. Oscar pulled himself to his feet and wandered over to rest his head against her knee. She stroked his ears as the interview commenced.

'Professor Pelletier? My name's Dan Armstrong and I'm helping Inspector Senese with the investigation into the murder of Nikolaos Diamantis.'

'I see. Are you English?'

'Yes, I am. Now, as far as Doctor Diaman—'

'Do you have a background in police work? You look like a copper to me.'

The slang term sounded so out of place, coming from somebody who spoke like Queen Elizabeth, that I couldn't help smiling. I nodded. 'Yes, I used to be a detective.'

'What were you? An inspector or something higher up the ladder?'

'I was a detective chief inspector at Scotland Yard. Now, if we can get—'

'And is this your lovely Labrador?'

'Yes, he's my do—'

'He's a very handsome dog.' Oscar shot her a glance that indicated that he was well aware of his good looks. 'What's his name?'

'Oscar, but I really—'

'But what are you doing here in Italy? Are you on holiday?'

'No, I live here. Now, please, if you don't mind, I need to ask *you* some questions. This is a murder inquiry, after all.' It was patently obvious that this lady had an inquisitive streak and I could see why Violet had recommended her to me as a fount of information. 'Can you think of anybody who might have been responsible for the death of Doctor Diamantis?'

'You mean from among the people here?'

'Anybody.'

I saw her pause for reflection for a few seconds. 'I really can't see anybody here doing anything as horrid as committing murder, but there's no doubt that Nikolaos was loved and hated in equal proportions.' She looked back at me and her green eyes sparkled. 'Mostly loved by the ladies and hated by the men.'

'Can you give me any names? I promise I won't reveal you as the source of the information.'

'Oh, I'm not worried about that. I'm far too old to be concerned about what people think of me. As for names, there are a number so I think I'd better divide them into aspiring conquests and those with whom...' she gave a very Gallic shrug of the shoulders '...with whom things had already become more intimate.'

I translated into Italian for the young policeman's benefit and saw his eyes roll. Oblivious or impervious to our reaction, Professor Pelletier held up one hand and started to tick the names off on her crooked fingers. 'Now, let me see... the names that come to mind in the hopeful category would have to include Juliette from Paris, Ingrid from Austria and Carla from Italy, although she's let herself go since I last met her, poor dear. I can't tell you whether anything already happened between any of them and Nikolaos but I definitely have the feeling they would have been willing partners if he had asked. Those with whom things were more serious are, to the best of my knowledge, Freja from Sweden, Monica from Manchester, and Pilar and Elena from Barcelona – either singly or both together.' As she mentioned the two Spaniards, she produced a positively roguish grin. By this time, she had started counting on the fingers of her other hand as well and Gori had almost worn his pen out.

I did my best not to let my amazement show in my voice. 'I make that three possibles and four probables. Nobody could accuse Doctor Diamantis of being shy as far as members of the opposite sex are concerned. It's a wonder he ever got any work done. My compliments, Professor Pelletier, on your memory and your investigative talents. My next question is whether you can think of any jealous boyfriends, girlfriends or husbands of any of these ladies.'

'As far as I'm aware there's only one husband here and that's Peter from Manchester. He's married to Monica, Monica Fowler. I believe Ingrid is also married, but she told me her husband's on an expedition to Nepal. I don't think any of the others are married but I might be wrong.'

'And boyfriends, jealous or otherwise?'

'None that I know of, although there are several men who chase after Freja – you've probably noticed them yourself. In particular, the tall Roman with the ponytail who's clearly got his sights set on her... Massimo Something-beginning-with-S, I think his name is. There might well be a few more because she can be a terrible flirt, especially after a glass or two of wine. I have a feeling he and Monica might have had a little fling as well, but I have no proof of that.'

I had a shrewd idea that Anna might not be surprised by the professor's description of Freja as a flirt but, out of a sense of solidarity with a fellow author, I added a question mark alongside this comment on my pad before moving on to the next on the list.

'And what about Monica's husband? Doesn't he mind that his wife's been carrying on with other men?'

'You'd better ask him yourself.' I got the feeling the diminutive professor knew more than she was disclosing about Monica's husband, but hopefully that would emerge in questioning.

I made a note of the names of the two men and underlined Peter Fowler, the Englishman married to Monica from Manchester, allegedly one of Nikolaos's conquests. Here, at least, we had a possible suspect with both opportunity – he was here – and a solid motive rooted in jealousy. With Professor Pelletier's help, we identified the surnames of the people she had mentioned and I thanked her for her cooperation. A quick check of the names on my list revealed that I would be interviewing Monica Fowler next to last, with her husband, Professor Peter Fowler, immediately afterwards. I had a feeling my interviews with this couple might prove to be interesting.

8

SATURDAY AFTERNOON

I sent Gori to Bruno and Virgilio with the other names mentioned by Professor Pelletier so that they could keep an eye out for them while I nipped outside with Oscar for a breath of air. We stayed close to the hotel as I didn't have much time to waste, but I made sure we kept clear of the murder scene. We went around to the far side of the property and carried on down a narrow, winding, gravel path towards a massive but meticulously trimmed box hedge that looked as if it had been there for centuries. On the other side of this was the hotel's vegetable garden and I found an elderly gentleman working there, preparing the ground for spring planting. I stopped for a quick chat and discovered that he lived in the nearby little town of Pontenuovo and came here to help out and to make himself a bit of extra money. From what I had heard, he was presumably the person who had discovered the body, although he was looking relatively untroubled at having seen such a gory sight. Still, I made sure I brought up the subject of the murder as gently as possible. His reply made clear what he believed to have happened.

'It's a terrible thing when a man can be torn apart by a pack of wolves just a few metres from a hotel full of people.' He was missing several teeth and as a result, he whistled slightly as he spoke.

I was glad Freja Blomqvist and Pavel Havel weren't here to hear this. Remembering what they had said about the risks of demonising an endangered species, I did my best to put the wolf attack rumour to rest. 'I've been speaking to the inspector in charge of the case and he's told me categorically that it had nothing to do with wolves, although he believes that the murderer wanted to give that impression as a way of throwing the police off the scent. Please tell your friends and neighbours that the murder here was definitely committed by humans, not wolves. Besides, I have it on good authority that wolves aren't a danger to humans anyway.'

He gave me a sceptical look. 'It's not your chickens they steal. And they take bigger animals, too. We found the remains of a deer just outside Pontenuovo last month and local farmers have lost lambs. If they can take a sheep or a deer, they can take a child. They should be killed off, not protected. Did you see the state of that poor man's body? A human being wouldn't do something like that to another human being.'

In my time at the Met, I had seen the gruesome results of what human beings could do to each other but this old boy had had enough of blood and gore for one day so I just repeated my words about wolves not being involved. He looked far from convinced and I left him grumbling to himself and I went back inside, reflecting that it was pretty clear that wolves had had a bad press around here and realising that feeling against them was running high. High enough for murder? Could it possibly be that somebody had decided to kill one of the conservationists out of spite, or as a pretty radical way of raising awareness of what they perceived to be the wolf threat? But who would be prepared to go to such lengths over the loss of a few farm animals? My thoughts returned momentarily to Reiner and Suzy. Had they lost any of their chickens? Might that have made a sociopath like him angry enough to want payback from the scientists responsible for the protection of the wolf here in Tuscany?

When Oscar and I got back inside, the interviews continued. Almost all of these passed quickly without adding anything useful to our inquiry. Most people appeared to be shocked and saddened by what had happened and I was unable to identify any signs of guilt. However, when it was the turn of Monica from Manchester, I was especially interested to hear what she would say.

Doctor Monica Fowler was a good-looking woman. If Professor Pelletier was right and she had had an affair of some kind with the dead man, I would have expected her to look saddened, maybe even distraught. Instead, her face was expressionless. To an old sceptic like me, this lack of reaction didn't necessarily prove innocence. It could be a façade and consequently equally suspicious, considering that virtually every other person we had interviewed had been visibly upset and several had even shed tears.

I started with the standard questions and learned that she worked in the entomology department of Manchester University where she had a special interest in bees. I wasn't surprised to hear her say that she couldn't think of anybody who might have borne a grudge towards the Greek. This had been a recurring theme in all the interviews but I had a feeling she knew more than she was letting on, so when it became clear that she wasn't going to offer any information voluntarily, I decided to take the bull by the horns.

'I understand that you and Doctor Diamantis were close. I'd be grateful if you would tell me how close you were to him and, Doctor Fowler, please bear in mind that this is a murder inquiry. We're recording what you say, and you may be required to repeat it under oath.' I made sure I sounded as formal and solemn as possible in an attempt to shake her out of her uncommunicative stance. After a brief delay, I was relieved to find that it did. Her shoulders slumped and her eyes dropped to her clasped hands.

'We were *very* close, Inspector.' I had no idea who had told her of my former career but presumably the delegates had been chatting amongst themselves as the interviews proceeded. 'I'd known Nico on and off for five years and I was immediately drawn to him when I first met him.' She looked up and her impassive expression had been replaced by cheeks glowing with embarrassment and the sparkle of tears at the corners of her eyes. 'Nico and I were lovers.'

'For five years?'

She shook her head. 'No, only since last autumn.' She gave a heartfelt sigh.

'You're based in Manchester?' I saw her nod and I continued. 'But I believe Doctor Diamantis was living in Switzerland, so presumably you didn't have many opportunities to meet. After all, you are married, aren't you?'

To my surprise, she gave a dismissive wave of the hand. 'Peter doesn't count. He and I have been living separate lives for years now. He has his friends and I have mine.'

'Did he know about you and Doctor Diamantis?'

'Maybe... probably. I've no idea. I never mentioned Nico to him by name but Peter knew I had other male friends.'

'When you say, "other male friends", does this mean that you have other male lovers apart from the victim?'

Her cheeks were still glowing red, but a harder note entered her voice and she stared at me defiantly. 'Yes, Inspector, that's exactly what I mean.'

A thought occurred to me. 'And are any of them here this weekend?'

She hesitated just a little bit too long before answering. 'No.'

I tried pressing her for more but this was all I could get out of her for now, so I moved on with the questioning. Her answer when I asked if she could account for her movements between dinner and breakfast led to an interesting revelation.

'I went straight up to my room, did some work and then went to bed.'

'Presumably your husband can vouch for that?'

She shook her head. 'My husband and I occupy separate rooms. I'm afraid I have nobody who can provide me with an alibi but I can assure you of one thing, Inspector: I would never have even considered hurting a single hair on Nico's head. Like I told you, I loved him.'

Once the door had closed behind her, I looked across at Gori. I thought it only fair to involve him in the investigation and I was interested to hear what he had to say. 'What did you think of Doctor Fowler? Do you think she might have done it?'

I saw him pause for reflection before answering. 'I tended to believe her when she said she loved him and I also believed her about the weird sort of marriage she's involved in, but whether that love could have turned to hate would depend very much on what the cause might have been.'

'Bravo, Gori, now think carefully, did you at any point get the impression she might be lying?'

This time he answered immediately. 'Yes. When you asked if she had any other boyfriends here and she said no. I believe that might well have been a lie.'

I reached over and patted him on the shoulder. 'My thoughts entirely. I think we would do well to keep a close eye on this lady and her friends and associates. Now, let's see what the husband has to say.'

Professor Fowler was the final interviewee on my list and he came as a surprise. From the way his wife had been talking, I had

been expecting a frail, older man, but such was not the case. He
was probably only a year or two older than her, maybe in his late
forties, tall with broad shoulders and he looked fit. My immediate
thought was that he would unquestionably have had the strength
to pick up a club or a hammer or something similar and deliver a
hefty blow to the victim's head. I indicated that he should sit down
opposite us and started the questioning.

'You are Professor Peter Fowler?'

'I am.'

'And you work at the University of Manchester like your wife?'
He nodded so I went on. 'Please would you tell me what your
subject is?'

'I'm the head of the crop science department and my own
personal area of research is GM crops.' Although I knew what he
was talking about, I let him explain, as much for the sake of
hearing how he spoke and seeing how he acted as anything else.
'We've been working to develop varieties of genetically modified
corn, which will be resistant to many of the parasites and diseases
that can destroy harvests in the developing world.'

Although he was at the University of Manchester, he had a
London accent. He sounded as though he was keenly interested in
his work and, at least for the moment, I could detect no signs of
unease or guilt in him. But, of course, maybe he was just a very
good actor. I'd met quite a few of them over the years.

'As you know, we're investigating the murder of Doctor
Diamantis. Did you know him?' I kept my eyes closely on his face
as I mentioned the victim's name but, again, I noted nothing
untoward.

'Just by sight. I believe he's... he was a specialist in fish or
marine animals. Not really my field of interest. Have you any idea
why he was killed?'

Again, nothing suspicious. 'That's what we're trying to ascertain. We're asking everybody this: please could you confirm where you were between the end of dinner last night and breakfast this morning.'

'I went to the bar with a bunch of other people after dinner and was there until about eleven o'clock.' I thought I detected the slightest hesitation before he added, 'After that, I went up to my room and I went to sleep.'

I decided to plead ignorance of the open marriage his wife had described. 'Can your wife confirm that?'

He shook his head. 'I'm surprised she didn't tell you. We're a married couple in name only. It suits us both to remain married but here, as at home, we lead separate lives and occupy separate rooms.'

'When you say that it suits you both to maintain a charade of being married, could you just explain what you mean by that?' I could see the annoyance on his face and so I added the usual proviso. 'I'm sorry, but this is a murder investigation and we sometimes have to ask awkward questions.'

'I can't see what it has to do with you or this investigation but it's quite simple really: we have two teenage daughters and for their sake, we've decided to stay together, at least until they've both left the nest.' He looked across and caught my eye. 'Listen, Inspector, I know my wife has been having other relationships and it doesn't bother me. For all I know, she might have been having a relationship with Diamantis, but I neither know nor care.'

'Thank you, Professor Fowler. Tell me, do *you* also have other relationships?'

I felt sure there was another momentary hesitation. 'Yes, from time to time, but nothing serious.'

'With anybody who's here this weekend?'

He shook his head, but I wasn't convinced. He, like his wife, would bear close observation.

9

SATURDAY LATE AFTERNOON

When I emerged from the interviews, it was to find that Bruno, assisted by Anna, still had half a dozen people to see so I decided to take Oscar for a decent walk. First I went upstairs to change shoes and was helped by Oscar, who ran off to pick up one of my trainers, which he brought back and dropped at my feet. I sat down on the end of the bed, pulled off one shoe and replaced it with the trainer while he went off and brought me the other one. This little ceremony was something we often did. In the wet winter months, he had occasionally brought my muddy wellingtons up to my bedroom. While I had appreciated the gesture, I hadn't appreciated having to clean up afterwards.

I went over to the window and pulled the sashes open. Our bedroom faced west and the late afternoon sun flooded in. I rested my elbows on the warm window ledge and looked across to where I thought I had seen a shadowy figure the previous night. Oscar, ever curious, stood up on his hind legs beside me and I could hear him sniffing the air with interest. It now appeared clear that wolves had not been involved in the death of Doctor Diamantis so, if I really had seen movement, it had almost certainly been of human origin and, equally probably, might have been the murderer. I noted the precise location between two large bushes and decided to investigate further.

We went out through the hall and walked around the side of the hotel to the back garden. Blue tape indicated that the area was still out of bounds but the officer on duty recognised me by now and even lifted the tape so I could take a look around. I told Oscar to walk to heel – something he had been getting better at recently – and I made my way across to the point I had mentally marked. This was between a huge clump of rosemary, taller than I was, and a prickly, spiny bush whose identity eluded me – botany has never been my strong point. Behind them was a gravel path that curled back towards the hotel again. Forensics had already discarded the idea that the victim might have been knocked unconscious elsewhere, as there were no signs of the Greek having dragged himself or having been dragged onto the lawn. In consequence, it was likely that his aggressor had either been with him and known to him as he stood on the grass in the bright moonlight or had been hiding behind either of these conveniently dense bushes from where he or she had sprung out to launch the attack.

I tried to visualise once again the movement I had spotted last night and the more I thought about it, the more it seemed clear to me that I had indeed seen somebody, rather than something. Assuming that this somebody had in fact been the murderer, it also seemed logical that this same person had managed to produce a creditable impersonation of a howling wolf, presumably in an attempt to add weight to the wolf-attack scenario. Unfortunately, I only had the vaguest idea of the fleeting figure I had seen, and there was no way I could even begin to guess whether it had been male or female.

As Oscar wandered about, I was turning over in my head the fact that this murder had without doubt been premeditated and meticulously prepared, even down to the murderer carrying two weapons: a club to knock the Greek out and a broken bottle so as to rip out the victim's throat. Had this meticulous preparation even included a crash course on wolf impersonation? And of course, I reflected, the fact that Oscar hadn't reacted to the spooky howl the previous night had been because it hadn't been a real howl. Presumably he could tell a fake when he heard it.

Although Oscar and I both sniffed around for a few minutes, we found no clues and in the end, I gave up and we set off up the usual track through the vineyards before branching off through the vines and circling back towards the hotel again. After ten minutes or so, we came to a patch of woodland where he could run around to his heart's content and find as many sticks for me to throw for him as he wanted. It was remarkably warm for early April and I was glad I hadn't bothered to put on a jacket. Somewhere in the distance, I could hear a woodpecker's laughing call and, apart from that, it was wonderfully peaceful here. But was it only an illusion of tranquillity? Could it be that the murderer would strike again?

As I played fetch with Oscar, I thought back over the people I had just interviewed and couldn't think of anybody else to put into the possible suspect category apart from the couple from Manchester, individually rather than jointly. The other interviewees had seemed genuinely shocked by the death of the Greek and I felt it was probably safe to dismiss them – at least for now. As for these two, could it be that Monica had seen Nikolaos Diamantis with another woman the previous night and had followed him outside to kill him in a fit of jealous rage? What he had been doing out in the garden in the middle of the night, however, remained a mystery. Her husband, on the other hand, in spite of what he had told us, might not feel the same way about their open marriage as his wife, and maybe he had killed the Greek out of jealousy.

Alternatively, if Monica – who had confessed to having other partners – had been having an affair with another of the symposium participants as well as Diamantis, might that man have killed Nikolaos to rid himself of a rival for her affections? Whatever the motive, both definitely needed to remain on the suspects list and we needed to discover the identity of Monica's other lover or lovers.

We stayed in the woods for a while where Oscar was in his element, charging into the undergrowth and coming back with sticks, pine cones, and anything else he could find for me to throw for him to retrieve. Finally, I checked the time and headed back towards the hotel with him running off into the vines to look for more objects for me to throw for him. As it seemed likely to me that the murderer had most probably exited and returned to the hotel through the French windows by the bar rather than running the gauntlet of being seeing by the night porter at the reception desk, I deliberately chose that way myself. After all, there was every likelihood that the killer would have had blood on his or her hands, if not on other parts of the body or clothing.

We were walking back through the garden towards the terrace and the French windows when Oscar suddenly disappeared into the bushes and emerged with something unusual in his mouth. He settled down on the path, gripped it between his front paws and set about chewing it to bits. Knowing that his insatiable appetite had already caused him to almost choke himself on objects as varied as a most unsavoury old shoe and a child's headless doll, I hastily crouched down and tried to wrestle it out of his mouth before he swallowed it. This involved a fair old tussle with him as anything he deems even vaguely edible goes straight down the hatch. Finally, I managed to pull it out of his powerful jaws and he jumped to his feet and stood there, front legs splayed, panting excitedly, waiting for me to throw it for him. But I didn't. Instead, I located a stick and lobbed it across to the other side of the lawn while I studied what he had found.

It was clearly a piece of wood and, equally clearly, it had been hand carved. It was the size and shape of a small ice-cream cone and somebody had taken the trouble to hollow it out. I hadn't got a clue what it was. It varied in thickness from a centimetre or so at the thin end to the width of an espresso coffee cup at the other. Interestingly, considering it had been lying under a rosemary bush, it was remarkably clean – apart from a liberal coating of Labrador drool – and so, after shaking out a reluctant spider who had set up home inside the hollowed-out tube, I put it to my lips and tried blowing.

The result was astounding. To my amazement, the sound that emerged from this small piece of wood was a loud, lupine howl. There could be no doubt about it; Oscar had found a vital piece of evidence, almost certainly dropped into the bushes by the killer in an attempt to dispose of it. Sadly, in pulling it out of Oscar's unwilling jaws, I had now covered it with my fingerprints as well as slobbery Labrador toothmarks and I had little doubt that any prints belonging to the murderer would have been smudged and impossible to retrieve. My thoughts were interrupted by Oscar's return with the stick I had thrown for him and I hastily threw it for him again while I pushed my way between the rosemary bush and a huge camellia bush in the direction from which he had originally emerged with his find.

In fact, it was remarkably easy to find what I was looking for and I had Oscar to thank for it. He came charging up behind me with the stick in his mouth and the damn thing caught me behind the knee and it stopped both of us in our tracks. As I bent down to massage my calf and mouth a few expletives I found myself confronted by pieces of broken glass littering the ground in front of me. It was brown glass and in the midst of it was the neck of a broken beer bottle. Making sure that Oscar kept his distance for fear of either cutting himself, destroying evidence or both, I crouched down and studied the pieces carefully. I didn't have a magnifying glass but I didn't need one to see what was unmistakably dried blood smeared on several of the sharper pieces. Between us, it looked almost certain that my dog and I had found the weapon used to tear the unconscious man's throat to shreds. I searched around for the club or other heavy object used to hit Diamantis but found nothing. No doubt that had been discarded elsewhere.

I took a couple of photos of the find before looking around and spotting one of the police officers I recognised. He was now wearing a disposable suit and was poking about on the far side of the garden. I waved to attract his attention and he came over at once. I stood alongside him as he slowly and carefully picked up the pieces with his gloved hands and slipped them into an evidence bag. When we were both sure that there was nothing more to be seen, I took the bag from the officer and led Oscar up onto the terrace to look for Virgilio and Bruno. I found them sitting outside in the sunshine. There was no sign of Anna or Lina. Presumably, they had left the detectives to discuss the case. I set the bag of broken glass fragments on the table and told them where Oscar and I had found them. Bruno beamed at me.

'Excellent, presumably the perpetrator dumped the bottle there for fear of it being found in his room if there were to be a search. Let's hope he wasn't wearing gloves and that we manage to get some prints off the glass.' He called across to the young officer who had been my companion earlier, who was standing a bit further along the terrace, sipping a coffee. 'Gori, call Forensics and tell them we're pretty sure we have the murder weapon and then jump in the car and deliver this bag to them as soon as possible. Be sure you look after it as carefully as if it was a newborn baby.' He bent down to ruffle Oscar's ears. 'Who's a clever dog, Oscar?'

Oscar just licked Bruno's hand. He already knew the answer to that one.

Virgilio was thinking aloud. 'Of course, if Forensics do manage to find prints, this means we'll have to fingerprint everybody in the hotel, and that's going to take time. I suppose we should start by taking prints from our prime suspects.' In response to my inquiring look, he pointed to the open notebook on the table in front of him. 'The way Bruno and I see it, there are probably no more than a dozen persons of interest who will require further questioning. The majority of the delegates are in the clear either because they have alibis or because we just didn't believe them to be capable of murder. As far as we can tell, none of the hotel staff are likely to have been involved although there are two of them – the night porter and a cleaner – who were up and about at that time.'

I nodded. 'I've only got two definites: Monica and Peter Fowler.' I went on to tell them about the couple's open marriage and my suspicions. 'So I think we definitely need to keep an eye on them, and you'd better add Massimo something-beginning-with-S as a result of what Professor Pelletier told me. It sounds as though he was keen on Freja and maybe Monica Fowler as well, so if Diamantis was also interested in these two women then we might have jealousy as a motive. Who's on your list?'

Bruno answered. 'I got Forensics to do a search of the victim's room and they've come up with a number of discoveries. Firstly, his bed hadn't been slept in, so that means he wasn't entertaining any ladies in his own room last night. Presumably, he must have been in somebody else's bed unless he just spent a few hours wandering around in the dark, which seems unlikely. In his room, there was a phone and a laptop, which are being studied as we speak.' He glanced across at me. 'If we run into language problems, maybe you'd be prepared to help out. His wallet was also still there so he evidently wasn't planning on going any great distance when he went outside.'

'What about the victim's social media? Is anybody looking into that?'

'Yes, but if you have a few minutes to trawl through it as well, that will be a big help.'

'Of course, I'll take a look this evening. I suppose the big question is what he was doing out there in the garden in the first place.'

Bruno had an answer to this. 'Take a look at this. It's the most interesting thing they found in the victim's room. It was crushed up in the waste bin.' He passed his phone across to me and showed me a photo of a crumpled piece of paper no bigger than a postcard and clearly torn from a larger sheet of lined paper. On it were a handful of words, handwritten in English in red ink:

MUST SEE YOU. BACK GARDEN AT 2.

There was no signature, but below it, the writer had drawn a funny little heart with an arrow through it. 'I've sent it off to Forensics in the hope that we can get some prints off it as well.'

I took a closer look at the handwriting. Back at Scotland Yard, I had sometimes employed the services of a graphologist called Mrs Connelly. This unassuming elderly lady produced results that in some – but not all – of the cases were little short of amazing. Not only could she almost always identify the gender of a writer and whether they were left- or right-handed, she could also come up with an estimate of the writer's age and often this proved to be uncannily close to reality. I remembered one particular occasion when the graphologist deduced that the writer of the note had been a man working in the IT industry, and when we caught the perpetrator, he turned out to work for a multinational software company. Not having the services of Mrs Connelly with me now, I did my best to remember what she had taught me.

The fact that the note was written in capitals made things more difficult. From the slight right to left inclination of the cross stroke on the T, it looked as though the person who had written it had probably been left-handed, and from the very precise way the number two had been written, it was a fairly safe bet that the writer had been a mathematician or scientist. The little heart would appear to indicate that the writer had been a woman, and one romantically linked to the victim, but that was all. I smiled ruefully after I had told the two detectives all I had been able to deduce.

'Not really an awful lot of help, but I suppose it's something.'

Bruno took up the saga. 'Every little helps. Thanks, Dan. As for suspects, the names that stand out, apart from your husband and wife from Manchester, are Massimo Santini as you said, Pavel Havel, Thomas Cartwright, Freja Blomqvist, Juliette Dujardin, Ingrid Schmidt Carla Vespucci, Hans Meyer and Dominic Green- grass. There are also the two Spanish ladies you mentioned, Dan, but they share a room and claim that they were both tucked up in bed all night.' He set down his notebook and reached for his coffee. 'It remains to be seen who with.'

I had been scribbling down his list of names as he reeled them off and I stared down at them. With the addition of the Fowlers, the total came to thirteen. I recognised almost all of the names: Massimo Santini had to be the name beginning with S mentioned by the French professor, Pavel Havel was the red-haired poo fancier and Thomas Cartwright, the supercilious Englishman whose squabble with the victim we had witnessed out on the terrace the previous afternoon. Carla Vespucci was, of course, the woman with the tortoiseshell glasses who had shared the award last night and who might have lusted after Diamantis if Professor Pelletier was right. Juliette's and Ingrid's names had also popped up on the French professor's list of possible candidates for the victim's favours, as had the two Spaniards', but the two men at the end were new to me, and I queried who they were. Bruno explained.

'Hans Meyer from Zurich and Dominic Greengrass from Dublin were seen by the night porter walking about – separately, not together – around the time of the crime. We have no reason at the moment to believe they were involved in the murder and are struggling to find any connection between them and the victim, but they definitely warrant further investigation.'

'What about CCTV? Any sightings of people entering or exiting rooms they shouldn't have been in?'

Bruno shook his head. 'Alas, the only cameras are in the entrance hall on the ground floor. Nothing upstairs at all. I've got people going through the footage but it looks as though the only people who came through the hall after midnight were the two staff members and Meyer and Greengrass. The bad news is that there are no fewer than three staircases and the French windows in the bar were unlocked all night, and indeed were wide open for an hour or so as the cleaner worked there, so anybody could have come downstairs, gone out and come back again without being observed.'

That appeared to confirm my hunch that the killer had used the French windows as a means of getting out of the hotel unseen. I shot a query at the inspector.

'The pathologist reckoned the victim bled to death. Would there have been a lot of blood on the murderer's clothes and body?'

'She says that if he was knocked unconscious, the killer could easily have slit his throat and then inflicted the other lacerations without getting contaminated.'

'So no help there, then. What about the neighbours? Did your people find anything of interest in the nearby houses and farms?'

'The fact of the matter is that there are very few nearby properties.' Bruno consulted his notebook again. 'Two holiday homes, both owned by foreigners and all locked up and empty, and three farms. The smallholding to the west of us is owned by a couple in their eighties and the sergeant who interviewed them said he reckoned they would have trouble lifting a bucket of milk after milking their one and only cow, let alone knocking somebody down and slashing them to pieces. On the other side of the big hill are your two friends, the Austro-American couple. My men who visited them report that they are a seriously strange couple who've been living in Italy for years but who speak less Italian than I do English.'

This didn't surprise me. 'They're certainly weird, all right, or at least the husband is. He told me they made the decision four years ago to drop out of the rat race, so they abandoned life in New York for solitude over here. I got the feeling that the decision was made by the husband rather than by both of them and I'm not so sure that his wife's as deeply into the whole cutting-themselves-off-from-civilisation thing as he is. As far as speaking Italian's concerned, they probably don't see any other living human beings from one week to the next, so that means they hardly ever need the language. I didn't see a phone or a TV in their house and, in fact, it looked as though they don't even have an electricity supply. Did your officers manage to get all the answers they needed or would you like me to call in on them?' I rather hoped the answer to that would be no, but I was to be disappointed.

'I'd be very grateful if you would, Dan, thanks. Just check where they were last night, any links with people here, you know the score. No rush, tomorrow will be fine. The only other farm is just along from the main entrance to the hotel grounds. It's slightly more interesting in that the man who owns it, Giorgio Carbonaro, claims he was woken last night, just like he has been on previous nights, to find wolves trying to get at his chickens. Apparently, the beasts regularly howl outside his window and he hates the damn things. If we're looking for somebody with a grudge against wolves, then look no further.'

I suddenly remembered the wolf-howl simulator that Oscar had found and dug it out of my pocket. 'That reminds me, take a look at this. Ever seen one of these before? Oscar found it in the same area as the broken bottle, just by the steps to the terrace.' I let them play with it for a few moments before picking it up and making it howl for them. This produced mixed results. Both detectives smiled, but then shook their heads ruefully when I explained that a combination of Oscar's teeth and my frantic efforts to tear it away from him before he swallowed it meant that there was no chance of getting fingerprints off it. It also attracted the attention of none other than Freja Blomqvist, who came rushing out of the French windows at the sound of the howl. When she saw the wooden object in my hands, she came over to the table with an eager expression on her face.

'What's that you've got there, Dan? Could I take a closer look? For a moment, I thought it was a real wolf.'

'I imagine that was the intention of whoever made it.' I passed it over to her. 'Have you ever seen something like this before? We believe it may have been used by the murderer.'

She shook her head. 'No, I've never seen one, but I've heard about them. Back in the days when wolves were hunted here in Europe, they used this sort of caller to bring them out of the forests.'

'Any idea where it's from? What nationality?'

'I really don't know. I suppose it could be Italian or maybe from one of the countries where they have the bigger, potentially more dangerous wolves, or in places like Slovakia where hunting is either still permitted or was only clamped down on quite recently.'

'And which countries might those be?'

'Most probably the wilder parts of the former Eastern Bloc or Russia itself but, like I say, it's just a guess.'

After she had handed back the caller and gone off, Bruno glanced across the table. 'We don't have any Russians, but we do have a Czech, and he has a special interest in wolves. I think we'll have to show this to Doctor Havel, don't you?'

I nodded in agreement but I hadn't forgotten that Freja Blomqvist, the other wolf expert, hadn't looked as surprised as all that to hear there had been a murder. Was Uncle Jack carrying a big secret around with her?

10

SATURDAY EVENING

Anna was waiting for me when I got back to the room and she didn't waste any time. No sooner had I closed the door behind me and Oscar than she started. 'I've just been having a heart-to-heart with Lina... or, at least, she's been pouring out her heart to me.'

'It's about Virgilio's job, isn't it?' There was no need to wait for her to nod. 'I've never noticed it before, but today there have been several occasions when I've spotted something on her face. I've always envied them the way she's managed to accept the constraints of his job but it sounds as though she's reaching breaking point.'

'I really think she is. She was in tears, poor thing. I have no doubt she's still in love with him, but she's finding it harder and harder to compete with his job.'

I shook my head sadly. 'God, it's all so familiar, but what can we do?'

'I think it's a matter of what *you* can do, Dan. You know Virgilio really well now, and I know he trusts you. You've been through all this before so I think the best thing will be for you to sit down and talk to him. From what I could see this afternoon, I don't think he's got a clue that she's as upset as she is.'

I sat down on the edge of the bed and Anna sat down beside me and laid her hand on my knee as she continued. 'I know you men don't like talking about this kind of thing but it's in his own interests after all.'

She was right. I owed it to Virgilio to talk to him and, hopefully, to get him talking to his wife as a result, but I wasn't looking forward to it. I didn't envy them what lay ahead but I knew I had to try. I put my hand on top of Anna's and gave her a little smile. 'Of course, I'll speak to him. He's really got to talk it through with Lina, though. That was the mistake I made. Helen and I just never talked about this kind of thing. Maybe if we had done, things might have turned out differently.' I gave Anna's hand a squeeze. 'But, of course, then I wouldn't have met you.'

She gave me a little kiss on the cheek and stood up, and Oscar stood up with her. 'Right, I've been sitting down all afternoon and I could do with a walk.' As usual, the magic word had Oscar bouncing up and down alongside her, so I got up as well and made a suggestion.

'Bruno wants me to call in on Reiner and Suzy to ask a few questions but I can do that in the morning.' Seeing her quizzical expression, I explained. 'No big deal, just language problems. The officers who went to interview them found it hard to get through to them, so I volunteered to go. Don't worry, you're in the clear. I'll just go over and be in and out in five minutes. As far as now's concerned, why don't we walk along to the farm just up the road that makes the wine so I can buy Virgilio that bottle I owe him?'

Outside, the sun was low on the horizon behind us and we cast elongated shadows as we walked up the drive to the road. One of the things I love about Tuscany is the way generations of Tuscans have planted cypress trees alongside roads, tracks and drives and you can follow them for miles and miles as they stretch out across the hillsides. As we walked, Oscar ran ahead of us, as always in search of branches or pine cones. I reached across and caught hold of Anna's hand.

'You're sure you didn't mind my helping the inspector this afternoon? The last thing I would ever want to do would be to put you in the same situation that Lina now finds herself in.'

She squeezed my hand and shot me a little smile. 'You're forgetting that I was helping the inspector as well this afternoon but, don't worry, like I said before, I went into this relationship with my eyes open.'

'And you promise you'll tell me if you ever feel I'm putting work before you?'

'I promise, but I know there will be those times. It's normal, so don't worry.'

'How did it go this afternoon? Did it make you develop an urge to join the police?'

'It was interesting but, no, I'm very happy with my medieval history, thank you. Some of the people we spoke to were really upset at the death of Diamantis.' She gave me a little wink. 'And not just the women. By the way, did you realise that Doctor Diamantis was a bit of a celebrity?'

I shook my head. 'In what way? I heard that he was an authority on polar bears.'

'Apparently he was an Internet influencer, followed by tens of thousands on social media. They said he's been on TV and he produced a regular series of podcasts about environmental matters and he's interviewed quite a few big names in the field.'

'That's interesting.' If the victim had had wide exposure on the Internet, it was highly likely that he would also have racked up not only a legion of fans but also a number of climate-change deniers, weirdos and just plain angry people. Could it be that one of these might have infiltrated the symposium or had somehow managed to get into the hotel and lure Diamantis outside to his death? It occurred to me that there were a dozen or so people here at the hotel, apart from the four of us, who were simple guests, not connected with the symposium. I hadn't been involved with interviewing any of them and I wondered just how seriously Bruno might be considering them.

'What are you thinking?' Anna pulled me to a halt and stared at me closely, reaching up to tap me gently on the temples. 'I know that look. The computer's whirring away inside there, isn't it? Have you had a brainwave? Do you know who the murderer is?'

I smiled at her. 'I wish I did. As far as the brain's concerned, it's badly in need of a glass of wine to make it work better, but I was just thinking that maybe one of the other guests at the hotel might have had an interest in the victim which we've overlooked. My interviewees this afternoon were all scientists involved with the symposium, but there are some non-scientific guests like we are, the people who sit in our part of the dining room at mealtimes. Did you and Bruno interview any of them?'

'No, not as far as I remember. That was left to his men, seeing as the random guests are all either Italian or they speak Italian. I can see where you're coming from with this. You think the murderer might be one of them, don't you?'

'I honestly don't know, but it's another line of inquiry we need to follow up.'

Giorgio Carbonaro's farm was more winery than farm. Although I saw a handful of pale white cows in one field and chickens in a run alongside the yard, it was clear that the whole focus of the place was on wine. In one open-sided barn, I saw two of those funny little narrow tractors that the locals used for running up and down between the rows of vines. A tin awning sheltered a couple of trailers, stained a deep blueish-purple colour by the grapes they had carried six months earlier during the *vendemmia*. Another shed was overflowing with plastic crates, also stained, no doubt used when the grapes were being picked. Huge, old, wooden double doors set in an ancient stone archway led into the cantina proper and a small door carved into one of these had a sign on it marked, *Entrata*.

I tapped politely on the door and we stepped inside. A man was bending over ahead of us doing something to one of a long line of huge, wooden barrels set up on their sides and he looked up as we came in. He was probably around my age but his leathery, tanned exterior showed that, unlike me, he had spent most of his life outdoors. I pointed to Oscar. 'Good evening, is it all right if we come in with the dog? He's very friendly, probably too friendly.'

'As long as he doesn't pee on the barrels, he's very welcome, as are you.'

He came across to us and we shook hands. Oscar obligingly stood up on his hind legs so the man could ruffle his ears. 'That's a handsome dog you've got here. Make sure he doesn't run into any of the wolves.'

I decided to feign ignorance. 'Are there really wolves around here?'

'I should say! The damn things keep me awake in the night trying to get at my chickens. Like I say, keep a close eye on the dog if you're out in the woods, especially after dark.'

I told him we were staying at the hotel for the weekend and he looked up.

'The police were here earlier on. They were saying that there's been a death at the hotel.'

I decided to avoid mentioning my involvement with the investigation. 'Yes, a horrible business. Let's hope the police catch the person who did it before too long.'

'I was speaking to one of the staff earlier and he said the police thought it might have been a wolf attack.' I wondered if he had been talking to the gardener.

I shook my head. 'No, the pathologist has confirmed that it was murder all right.'

He wasn't giving up easily. 'Are you sure? They're dangerous animals, you know, and the numbers have increased over the past few years.'

'No, definitely not the wolves.'

'So it was murder, was it? It must be a bit scary knowing that you might be living in the same building as a killer.'

I exchanged glances with Anna. 'It's a bit unsettling, but hopefully the police are on the case.' It didn't sound as if he was going to be able to add anything to the investigation so I reverted to the subject of wine. 'As far as wine's concerned, for now, I just want to buy one bottle of good red but I promise I'll come back on Monday or Tuesday to stock up with more wine before leaving.'

He insisted we taste before buying and led us over to a counter made of thick planks of timber laid across the tops of two barrels. He produced three glasses and three bottles of wine, two red and one white, from a battered old fridge.

We started with the cold white, which was extremely drinkable, and I made a mental note to stock up on a few bottles. Chianti is essentially a red wine area, although an increasing number of producers these days are also planting white grape varieties. They are still in a minority, though, and the choice is limited, so since settling over here, I'd got into the habit of buying a few bottles for my little cellar back home when I found a good white.

I drank all the wine in my glass – I wasn't driving anywhere after all, and it went against the grain to do that swirling-about-and-spitting-out thing the experts do – but Anna just sipped hers, shook her head, and let me move on to tasting the reds. Signor Carbonaro also downed the wine in his glass and then splashed a little red into my glass, swilled it about and jettisoned the wine onto the compacted earth floor of the cellar before half filling the glass and pushing it across the counter towards me.

'Good table wine, 12 per cent. You can drink as much of this as you like and I promise you'll still feel good next morning.'

I took that with a pinch of salt but had to admit that it was very good wine, quite a light red colour and certainly very drinkable. After I had made suitably appreciative noises and, of course, swallowed the lot, Signor Carbonaro refilled his glass and mine from the other bottle of red.

'Twenty-four months in oak barrels, 14 per cent. Strong and aromatic but needs to be treated with respect. I supplied six dozen bottles to the hotel for a wedding last summer and found one of the guests inside my chicken run next morning, fast asleep with one of the hens nesting in his trousers.'

'Talking of chickens, tell me more about these wolves.' Although I had heard the verdict of the scientists and the gardener at the hotel, I was interested to see how a real farmer felt about them. 'Are they dangerous to humans?'

'They say they aren't, but of course they are.' He pointed down to where Oscar was happily stretched out on the floor at my feet. 'A big male wolf is almost twice the size of your dog and, like any animal, when it gets hungry or angry, something that big can do a lot of damage. If you want my opinion, the government should change the law and exterminate the lot of them.'

'You're not allowed to shoot them, not even to protect your live-stock?' I've always been pretty good at appearing gormless. The fact that half the time I probably am no doubt helps me with that.

'Protected status. Nothing we can do apart from accepting the fact that we'll lose a percentage of our lambs and poultry each year. We're supposed to be reimbursed by the government, but you wouldn't believe how many forms we have to fill in first.'

'So you have sheep as well?' Anna was still nursing her glass of white wine.

He looked slightly embarrassed. 'Well, no, but I could have, couldn't I? I blame it all on the scientists. I don't know what world they live in, but they need to understand that wolves and humans can't coexist.'

'But how can you get the scientists to change?' I was interested to see if he would rise to the bait.

'When some of their own start getting killed by wolves, they'll understand. It's the only way.' This was pretty extreme language. Was there a darker side to this countryman?

'You sound like the people we were talking to yesterday. Maybe you know them: an elderly couple who live over on the other side of the hill.'

'The Germans? Yes, I know them.' His tone said it all but I gave him a little prod all the same.

'That's them.' All right, they were originally Austrian but, to a Tuscan farmer, German was evidently close enough. 'Don't you get on with them?'

'I hardly ever see them, nobody does. They could be on a witness protection scheme for all I know.'

'Do you think they've been bothered by wolves?'

'If they keep any livestock, they're bound to have been. Mind you, from the way they've let their vines and olives go to rack and ruin, I doubt if they keep any animals. They're just tourists...' From the scorn in his voce, it was clear that Signor Carbonaro's opinion of them was low.

I ended up buying one of each of the different wines and thanked him for the tasting. As Anna and I walked back towards the dying rays of the evening sun, I was turning over in my head what he had just said. Could it be that this friendly farmer or one of his colleagues might have decided to use the conservation symposium as a means to stage a phoney wolf attack that would force the government to reverse what they saw as a disastrous policy? Could the murderer have come from the farming community? And what about Reiner with his hatred of scientists? Was it possible that he had got wind of this symposium and had decided to make an example of one of them, with the added bonus of damning the wolves into the bargain?

When we got back to the hotel, we found Virgilio and Lina sitting on the terrace. I went over and presented him with a bottle of the two-year-old red and congratulated him on winning the bet. It was on the tip of my tongue to recount what the farmer had said and the suspicions his words had aroused in me but, thinking back to Lina's conversation with Anna earlier, I decided to keep that until I could get Virgilio on his own. Now was definitely not the time to be talking shop. He told me that Bruno had gone home but would be back first thing on Sunday morning to start the next round of questioning with the people who had aroused our interest today, and from then on, I did my best to ensure that the conversation steered clear of anything to do with the murder. Easier said than done.

When the sun finally disappeared below the horizon and the temperature started to drop once more, we all got up and went inside. I was rather hoping to be able to get Virgilio to myself but he and Lina disappeared upstairs together so all I could do for now was wait until another opportunity presented itself. Anna and I went up to our room, where Oscar immediately stretched out on the floor with a heartfelt sigh and was soon snoring contentedly. Anna disappeared into the bathroom for a long, hot bath and I picked up my laptop and typed in the name Nikolaos Diamantis. A second later, I found myself faced with page after page of references to the man and I settled down to read all about him.

The first thing I found was his website, and it was clear to see that conservation and the effects of global warming had been his main concern. From there, I moved on to Facebook and scrolled back over the last weeks and months, dipping in and out of his posts and checking out photos of endangered species, retreating ice caps and stranded polar bears on ice floes as well as weather-related disasters around the world until I was feeling totally demoralised. This was a man who was telling us that our days on this planet were seriously numbered. Every now and then, amid the gloom and doom, there were happier photos of meetings, conferences and even a few receptions and formal dances. The recurring feature of these was that inevitably the Greek was always surrounded by beautiful women. I checked them closely and one immediately leapt out at me. It was Freja from Sweden and she was draped all over him.

I was diverted from my studies by Anna's voice from the bathroom gently suggesting that I might like to join her in the bath. Any gloom and doom I had been feeling disappeared in an instant. Life was good again.

11

SATURDAY EVENING

I deliberately left Anna behind and went down to the bar at seven-thirty in the hope of being able to find Virgilio on his own. There was no sign of him but I wasn't alone for long. I had barely ordered a glass of Giorgio Carbonaro's white wine at the bar and sat down at a table with it when I felt a touch on my shoulder and turned to find myself looking straight into the beautiful blue eyes of the Swedish carnivorous mammal specialist, children's author, and close friend to the victim.

'Good evening, Uncle Jack.' In spite of my suspicions I gave her a friendly welcome.

'Hi, Dan, it's good to see you.' She leant over the table towards me and her neckline didn't leave very much to the imagination. Considering that the woman I loved was only a few floors above us, I averted my eyes and decided that the best thing would be to stick to science.

'I was talking to a neighbouring farmer earlier on and he told me he wishes wolves could be wiped out completely. Apparently, they take chickens and lambs from farms around here every year. I have to say I'm pleased the death of Doctor Diamantis can't be blamed on wolves otherwise that could be very bad publicity for them. How endangered are they?'

I pushed out a chair and she sat down opposite me, but at least that way she didn't need to lean over so much. My mum used to tell me I was easily distracted and she had a point.

Freja's face grew more serious. 'Really endangered. If the government were to reverse their protected status, it would be disastrous. If a story of a wolf killing a human were to get out to the media, it could be devastating, not just here in Tuscany but throughout Europe.'

I was interested to keep her talking and I was just wondering whether I should offer her a drink when Pavel Havel materialised by her side and handed her a glass of red wine. She bestowed a glowing smile upon him and pulled him down onto the seat beside her so she could give him a peck on the cheek. I was impressed to find that he not only didn't swoon at the contact, but he didn't even blush. The Czech was clearly made of strong stuff.

'Good evening, Inspector. Have you made any progress?'

I was about to protest but stopped myself. There seemed little point. Clearly, as far as the gathering was concerned, I was now 'Inspector' and that was that. I gave him my usual guarded answer. 'I believe Inspector Senese is following a number of leads and I understand he'll be back in the morning for some further interviews with persons of interest.' I decided that it wouldn't do any harm to do a little bit of stirring. 'I seem to remember seeing both of your names on that list so you'll probably be called in at some point.'

For a second or two, Doctor Havel's cheeks glowed redder than his hair. 'He doesn't think we could be involved, does he?'

I decided to plead ignorance, not least because I was only coincidentally part of this investigation and there might have been further developments, unknown to me. 'I have no idea. Why, are you involved?'

His face flushed even more. 'Of course not; how can you say such a thing?'

'I'm pleased to hear it. Tell me, were either of you particularly friendly with Doctor Diamantis?'

For a fraction of a second, the Czech's eyes flicked sideways towards his Swedish colleague before he shook his head. 'Not really. We both knew him, of course. I've certainly bumped into him at a number of these sorts of gatherings over the years, but we've never collaborated on any projects.' We both shifted our attention towards Freja, who shook her head.

'And I never worked with him either. Like Pavel, I knew the guy and I liked him but we weren't particularly close.'

Had Pinocchio been sitting in front of me, he would probably have poked my eye out with his nose. I've developed pretty good antennae over the years towards people who aren't telling the truth and, even if I hadn't seen the photo of her with the victim or been forewarned by Professor Pelletier of Freja's history with him, I would have known that she was being, as the politicians say, disingenuous. Or, in police talk, she was lying through her teeth. I toyed with the idea of calling her on this but saw no point in putting her on the spot this evening. That could safely be left to Bruno tomorrow morning. Besides, as I was about to remind Virgilio, we were on holiday.

At that moment, I spotted Virgilio emerging through the door at the far end of the bar. I hastily excused myself and went over to him. As far as I could see, he was on his own, so maybe the time for a tête-à-tête had arrived. I wasn't looking forward to it, but I knew it had to be done.

'Hi, Virgilio, what can I get you? This white wine's good. It's from the farm next door.'

He shook his head. 'I'm sure it must be great. I opened your bottle of red upstairs and tried it. It's excellent and thanks again, but I'll wait until we eat before I drink any more alcohol. I need to keep a clear head just in case anything else happens here this evening.'

I seized on this as my intro. 'Why do *you* need to keep a clear head? You're on holiday, after all.'

He smiled ruefully. 'You know how it is, Dan; in this job, we're never really off duty.'

'About that...'

But before I could launch into the speech I'd been preparing, he pointed across the room.

'There's Massimo Santini over there and he's on his own. Why don't we go over and have a little chat to him? He's the guy that the French professor told you maybe has the hots for Freja Blomqvist and/or Monica Fowler, isn't he? If one or both of them really were having an affair with the victim, then maybe this guy got jealous and killed Diamantis out of spite.'

'Yes, but it's not really up to us...' My voice tailed off as he was already on his way over to the tall Italian with the pigtail. Reluctantly, I followed him. When we reached Santini, the scientist greeted Virgilio with a smile.

'Good evening, Inspector, how's the investigation proceeding?' By now, I thought I could recognise a Roman accent when I heard one and I felt sure I could also recognise real interest beneath the apparently casual enquiry. Whether this was just natural curiosity or something more remained to be seen.

'Remarkably well, thank you.' Virgilio beamed at him. 'Inspector Senese tells me he's hopeful of being able to make an arrest as early as tomorrow.'

I studiously kept the surprise off my face. As far as I knew, the investigation still had a long way to go and certainly no prime suspects – at least not until we got any fingerprints from the broken bottle to match with somebody here. I understood what Virgilio was doing: just what I had been doing with Freja and Havel, stirring the pot to see if anything floated to the surface. I studied the Roman's face and thought I might even have seen something flit momentarily across it. Guilt? Shock? Apprehension? It was difficult to tell. He collected himself and produced a hearty response that still sounded less than sincere.

'Well, that's very good to hear. I hope it's not one of my colleagues. I can't believe that anybody here would commit murder.'

Virgilio kept it vague. 'I wouldn't know. It's not my investigation but it sounds promising.'

At that moment we were descended upon by Violet Grosvenor, the headmistress, and from the look on her face, she wanted something. 'Excellent, I've got both of you police officers here.' I was going to protest but she just sailed on with her interrogation and I let it go. Although I was no longer a police officer, I suppose she was right in that, like it or lump it, I had managed to get myself involved in this investigation. 'Please can you tell me if a decision's been taken about tomorrow's excursion to Siena? We've decided to cut it short and make it only lunch there – that's already booked – followed by a few hours in the afternoon to visit the city. That way, we can recoup most of today's cancelled sessions tomorrow morning. The thing is that the people at the coach company want to know tonight if we're going to need them or not.'

Virgilio nodded. 'I spoke to Inspector Senese about this and he asked me to tell you that he agrees to the excursion going ahead, but he requests that you travel as a group and that everybody returns together. Anybody who chooses not to go will still be expected to remain here at the hotel. He also asks if there will be space on each of the coaches for a couple of his men to accompany the group. At this point, it's still uncertain why Doctor Diamantis was killed, so there remains a risk, however slim, that the murderer may strike again.'

An expression of relief spread across Violet Grosvenor's face. 'Splendid news. Yes, of course, I'll make sure there'll be space for his men. Please thank him for his concern. I appreciate it.' Her face became more serious. 'I do hope this is the end of these horrible murders, though.'

I decided to float an idea past her and the Roman. 'I've been wondering whether maybe this murder might have been committed deliberately by somebody who was hoping that it would result in the death being blamed on wolves. I gather there's a lot of ill feeling among farmers about the way the wolves are multiplying and many of them would welcome a change in the law. What do you think?'

'You think somebody from outside might have done it to stir up popular opinion?' Violet Grosvenor sounded pleased. 'I'm sure that sounds like a much more likely scenario. I just can't begin to imagine how one of my colleagues here could do such a thing. Don't you think so, Massimo?'

'I'm a microbiologist, so I don't know much about mammals, but I'm sure you could be right. Certainly, wolves are viewed by many people, not just farmers, as being a menace. In the Apennines, not far from where I am in Rome, we often hear stories about lambs and even household pets being taken. I've even heard of them coming into the suburbs of some quite big towns.' He glanced across at Violet. 'Do they kill lots of animals every year? What about humans?'

Her reaction was the same as the two wolf specialists had produced. 'My field of interest is marine mammals, but I do know that, although wolves do take a certain number of lambs and poultry every year, they also do a good job of keeping down the wild boar and deer populations – and those animals do far more damage to agriculture. I also believe that most of the EU countries have a scheme to compensate farmers when they do lose livestock, so wolves aren't as bad as you might think, and I do know that they would never dream of attacking humans. I blame all the hysteria on horror movies.'

I spared a thought for my four-legged friend upstairs, no doubt snoozing happily at Anna's feet. I certainly wouldn't feel so tolerant if he were torn apart by wolves.

Meanwhile, Virgilio had returned his attention to the tall Roman. 'Tell me, Doctor Santini, have you any theories as to who might have murdered your colleague?'

He shook his head. 'I find it quite incredible, Inspector. I didn't know Nikolaos very well, but everybody said he was a nice guy. Why kill him?'

Why indeed?

At this moment, we were joined by Pavel Havel and I studied the faces of the two men closely. It was clear that Havel was close to Freja and, if Professor Pelletier was right and Santini was besotted by her, I was expecting fireworks, but I could sense no tension at all in the atmosphere as the two men met. Either the elderly French lady was mistaken or neither of the men felt as strongly about Freja as all that. Or they were both good actors.

It was clear that the opportunity for Virgilio to have a quiet one-to-one with Santini had now passed so he and I left them to it, and I steered him out onto the terrace, away from the crowd. It was noticeably cooler out here but not quite as cold as the previous nights. Spring was definitely breaking out all over. When I was certain that we were not in danger of being overheard, I launched into my subject, hoping I wasn't overstepping the bounds of friendship.

'Um, Virgilio, there's something I need to say to you.'

He must have picked up on my tone. 'What is it, Dan? Is something wrong? Trouble between you and Anna?'

'No, all good, thanks. It's not Anna I wanted to talk to you about; it's Lina.'

'Lina?'

'She and Anna have been talking. Well, to be honest, Lina's been pouring her heart out and Anna says it's clear that she's been getting increasingly unhappy.' I was quick to clarify. 'Not with you, just your work commitments.' I studied his face closely and was greatly relieved to read comprehension begin to dawn, so I took heart and soldiered on. 'I must admit that there were a couple of times today when I found myself being reminded of the way things became between me and Helen in our last years together. You're my best friend and I'd hate it for your marriage to go the same way mine did, so please don't take this the wrong way. I'm not trying to interfere with your personal life, I'm only trying to help.' I took a big mouthful of white wine and waited anxiously for his reply. It took quite a while but I was greatly relieved by what he said when he did start speaking.

'Thanks, Dan, and thanks to Anna. I appreciate you telling me this. I must admit it doesn't come as a complete surprise, but I suppose, to be honest, I've been ignoring it and hoping it would go away. I hadn't realised the extent to which it's got to her.' He held out his hands helplessly, palms upwards. 'What can I do? I know the job's the problem, but I love what I do. All right, I moan about it on occasions, but I wouldn't want to change it. Of course, there's no way I would ever want things to turn sour between me and Lina, but it's knowing what to do that's the problem. I suppose I could put in for a desk job where I could work a normal working week but you and I both know how that would end up. I'd be bored to tears within days. You know what it's like.'

And I did. My heart went out to both of them. It was all so

brutally familiar. Being married to a copper isn't easy. Apart from the unsociable hours, there's always the lurking fear in the mind of the partner back home that something awful will happen, like serious injury or even death. Although UK police are still mostly unarmed, gun and knife crime has been going up and up over recent years, and injuries to police officers have risen accordingly. Over here in Italy, even the local town bobbies who stick parking tickets on your windscreen carry weapons so it's even worse. I could fully understand how this constant worry could just grow and grow over the years until it became unbearable. At the same time, I knew exactly how Virgilio felt. I had enjoyed my job but, above all, it had made me feel useful, genuinely there to help people, and that was a good feeling. In the end, I had had to accept that my feelings for my job had been stronger than my feelings for my wife, and the divorce had been inevitable, but it had been tough for both of us.

'Listen, Virgilio, I'm the worst person to try to give you advice. Look what happened to my marriage. Ever since I've got to know you and Lina, I've envied you your happiness and I know that the last thing you would ever want to do is to jeopardise that. But you're going to have to sit down and talk it through with her. That's what I didn't do until it was too late. Your bond with Lina is too strong to break. Talk it over with her and I'm sure you'll be able to find a solution.'

In spite of my optimistic words, I wasn't so sure.

Dinner that night was a more sombre affair, not just because of the murder. Virgilio did his best to appear attentive and considerate to Lina, and Anna and I joined in, hoping to lighten the atmosphere. Even so, the strain on Lina's face was all too evident, and conversation around the table became ever more stilted. Finally, before the dessert arrived, she stood up and very politely excused herself, saying she had a headache. Virgilio looked uncertain for a moment but then jumped to his feet and followed her. I looked across at Anna and shook my head sadly.

'That was tough. I do hope they're going to be able to work through it. I managed to have a talk to him earlier on before you and Lina came along, but it's the same old story: job or wife?'

She reached across and caught hold of my hand on the table-top. 'Thanks for trying, I know you did your best. They're two really nice people and they deserve to be happy.' She smiled. 'Like we are.'

I felt a cold, wet nose nudge my ankle. For a moment, I wondered whether Oscar had worked out that we were going to have two spare desserts, and he was offering his services as an efficient waste-disposal system. I handed him down a breadstick and shook my head.

'No pudding for you, dog. How do you expect to outrun a wolf if I let you get tubby?'

From the look on his face, it was pretty clear that he was prepared to take his chances.

12

SUNDAY MORNING

I got up early on Sunday morning and went out for a walk with Oscar. It was noticeably warmer today but I spotted grey clouds on the horizon and I had a feeling that we would see rain before the end of the day. Hopefully, our visit to Siena wouldn't be rained off. Oscar and I headed in a different direction today and followed a track that curled up the wooded hillside to the south until we emerged into a clearing where somebody had thoughtfully placed a wooden bench at the side of the track. From here, I could look back down at the hotel and the surrounding vineyards. For now, the vines were still bare after the winter, but it would only be a matter of weeks before the whole area was green once more and the age-old cycle of growth, harvest and the magical transformation of the juice into wine would start up all over again. Yes, Tuscany definitely took some beating.

My phone started ringing but I didn't recognise the number. Still, maybe it was business so I answered it anyway. I discovered that it was Inspector Bruno Senese.

'*Ciao*, Dan. I hope you had a peaceful night. I've just heard from Virgilio that he's tied up this morning, but he gave me your number. I wonder if you're all right to help out when I interview the dozen or so persons of interest.'

I was pleased to hear that it sounded as though Virgilio was doing his best to convince Lina that she came first in his life by showing that he was prepared to ignore his natural instincts so as to be with her. 'Of course, I'd be happy to. By the way, when your men were interviewing the other guests, not those connected with the symposium, was there anybody of interest among them? This whole wolf business has got me thinking and I wondered whether it might be somebody with a grudge against wolves who staged the illusion of a wolf attack on purpose so as to generate bad publicity. Did they all seem reasonably normal people? Nobody with a strong agricultural background or a history of opposition to giving wolves protected status?'

There was a pause while I could imagine him flicking through the pages of his notebook. When he replied, he sounded intrigued. 'Good thought, Dan. Most of them seem fairly normal people: a couple of shopkeepers from Florence, a handful of pensioners from Milan and Bologna and a little group of birdwatchers from Venice, but there's one guy who works in the agriculture department of the university of Pisa. He's here with his girlfriend. I think I'll call him in for a second interview as well.'

'What time do you want to start? If it's not too early, I'll pop across to the Austrian couple first to ask the questions that they couldn't understand yesterday.'

'That would be great, thanks. Shall we say ten o'clock for the start of the interviews? That should give you ample time, shouldn't it?'

I confirmed that this sounded fine and he continued. 'By the way, I'm going to get fingerprints off everybody we sit down and talk to this morning. They've just called from the lab to say there are some partials on different pieces of that broken glass you found and they're busy trying to put them together into a decent set of prints to compare with these suspects. The note we found in the victim's room also has a few fragments of prints on it but nothing conclusive. Let's hope they can cobble something together from all the bits and maybe we'll find a match. If we don't, then I suppose we're going to have to fingerprint everybody here at the hotel, and that's going to take an age.'

After breakfast, I left Oscar with Anna and drove around to Reiner and Suzy's house. As before, I received a frosty greeting from the sheepdog and an even frostier one from his master.

'I didn't expect to see you again.'

'Me neither.' I told him why I had come, simply describing myself as the interpreter who had been roped in as I was staying at the Hotel dei Boschi Idilliaci where a murder had been committed, and he reluctantly invited me in. There was no sign of his wife, but the ginger cat was once more sprawled regally on the chair. I sat down and Reiner sat opposite me. Today, he didn't offer me a coffee but that didn't come as a surprise. From the look of him, it was all he could do to stay civil. I pulled out my notebook and rattled through the questions, starting with where he and his wife had been on Friday night. The answer was monosyllabic.

'Here.'

'Both of you?'

'Yes.'

'Were you aware that there was a scientific symposium taking place at the hotel?'

'No.' There was momentary hesitation before he exploded. 'Damn scientists. Just think of their carbon footprint, coming here from all over the world. It's disgraceful. They're destroying the planet.'

'It's actually a conservation symposium. I think you'll find these are the good guys.'

'There are no good guys when it comes to scientists. We'd be better off without them.'

The interview didn't last much longer and I was pleased to leave. As I drove back down the track away from the house, I wondered just how far he would be prepared to go to rid the world of his hated scientists.

* * *

I met up with Bruno at ten o'clock as agreed. Anna had declared herself quite happy for me to help out with the interpreting and questioning as long as I took Oscar with me while she went to the spa. She, too, was giving Virgilio and Lina space to spend time together and hopefully to talk things over. We had deliberately had breakfast in our room so as to stay out of their hair. Of course, the four of us would be lunching together in Siena and we couldn't change that, but this afternoon's tour of the city would be a perfect opportunity for Anna and me to go off and leave the other two to their own devices.

I gave Bruno my report on my fairly frosty conversation with Reiner and saw him nod.

'Do you think this guy might have been behind the murder?'

'I honestly don't know. He's an elderly man and he claims his only means of transport is a horse, so I think it's unlikely that he would have made it over here in the first place. If he did manage to get here, I seriously question whether he's crazy enough to commit murder. Yes, he's got some pretty radical views on scientists but, for example, I don't particularly like football hooligans but this doesn't mean I would go out and murder them. I think we definitely need to bear him in mind for now but, on balance, I doubt if he's our man.' I shot him a little smile. 'But I've been wrong before.'

Bruno thanked me and told me the questions he wanted to put to the people this morning – essentially quizzing them on their connections, romantic or otherwise, with the victim and double-checking where they had been that night and with whom – and he told me to feel free to ask whatever questions I wanted. I got the feeling he was glad to have my assistance and it felt good to know that my expertise was still required at the ripe old age of fifty-six and three quarters. I passed on a few thoughts I had had overnight.

'Virgilio and I had a brief chat to Santini last night and he told us he's a microbiologist and, as such, he doesn't know the first thing about wolves. This could mean he's the man who dreamt up this whole charade, not realising that wolves attacking humans would be most unusual. I have no doubt that whoever killed Diamantis deliberately set out to try to make it look as if he'd been attacked by wolves, in the hope of deflecting suspicion.' I went on to tell him about the photo I had found of Diamantis and Freja together before adding, 'Also, when I asked Freja yesterday how well she knew the victim, even Oscar could have heard the insincerity in her voice when she told me they weren't particularly close. I think these two will definitely need watching.'

'Absolutely, and your couple from Manchester also sound promising. Anybody else you're particularly interested in?'

'I'd like a chance to sit down and grill Thomas Cartwright. He's the guy involved in the argument Virgilio and I saw on Friday afternoon. I can't see why this would have made him go out and kill Diamantis but there was something about him I just didn't like, and I'd quite like to put him under a bit of pressure in the hope that he might reveal something of interest. I think he's hiding something. It's just a hunch.'

Bruno shot me a little grin. 'A detective's hunch? We all have them.'

Two of Bruno's men were stationed outside the interview room, charged with taking fingerprints from each of the intervie-wees before they came to see us. At my suggestion, everybody was also asked to print their name in capital letters on a list. Even without the help of Mrs Connelly, I hoped this might result in our being able to identify, or at least narrow down, who had written the note found in the victim's room.

Bruno started the interviews with one of the other 'normal' guests, not involved with the symposium. This was Doctor Vincenzo Albese from the University of Pisa and when he came into the room, I realised that he was the guy whose girlfriend had been attempting to eat oysters on the next table on the first night. He looked puzzled and slightly nervous but I couldn't see any sinister signs of guilt in him. He was probably about the same age as the victim and he told us he was a lecturer in food science. He told us his sphere of interest was principally oil-producing plants ranging from oilseed rape, through corn and palm oil, to olives. As such, he had nothing to do with carnivorous mammals. We pretty quickly ruled him out of our enquiries as we couldn't see what he could possibly have to gain from giving wolves a bad name but, just before leaving, he provided an interesting snippet of informa-tion when Bruno asked him if he'd noticed anything unusual or suspicious on Friday night.

'I'm sorry, it didn't occur to me when I was talking to the other officer yesterday, but there might be something. I didn't *see* anything, but I did hear raised voices in the corridor outside our room in the middle of the night. The noise woke me up.'

'And what time would that have been?'

'Just before two o'clock in the morning. I looked at my watch.'

'Could you hear what the argument was about? Any idea who it was?'

He shook his head. 'I'm sorry, it sounded like two men, and they were talking in English. My technical English is reasonable, but I couldn't make out what they were saying. Sorry.'

'And you have no idea who they were?'

This time, his answer was more helpful. 'I'm in room twenty-nine and opposite me are two doors: twenty-eight and thirty. When the argument ended, I heard a door close and it had to be one of those, but I couldn't tell which.'

After he had left, Bruno consulted the room list produced by the hotel, which revealed that room twenty-eight was occupied by Thomas Cartwright and room thirty by Massimo Santini. Had these two men been arguing in the corridor or had somebody else come along to argue with one of them before returning to his own room? And what had the argument been about?

The next few interviewees produced nothing very useful. These were Juliette Dujardin, Carla Vespucci and Ingrid Schmidt, all of whom had been named by Professor Pelletier as possibly having been romantically inclined towards the victim. All three acknowledged that they had found him attractive but stipulated that nothing had happened between them. Ingrid, in particular, was most insistent on that, swearing that she would never be unfaithful to her husband. Carla, with her thick glasses and severe hairstyle, didn't look like the sort to be prepared to jump into bed with a known womaniser like Diamantis and, of the three of them, she looked the least upset at his death – but murder affects people in different ways. Maybe she was mourning internally.

These three were followed by a more interesting pair: the two Spanish lecturers from the University of Barcelona, Pilar and Elena. Pilar, the first to be questioned, revealed nothing more than that she had spent the night in the room she shared with Elena, but when her friend was interviewed, she very quickly confessed that a lot more than that had been going on. Apparently, the two ladies had spent several hours in bed with the Irishman, Doctor Greengrass.

When we interviewed him, he freely admitted that he had happily hopped into bed with these two and had returned to his room around two-thirty – no doubt with a smile on his face. When asked if he had seen anybody or heard anything untoward during or after their tryst, he shook his head and told us that when he had left the Spanish ladies' room, he had gone downstairs to collect his briefcase and then had gone straight back up to his room.

Our next interviewee was the other person spotted wandering around the corridors in the middle of the night: Doctor Hans Meyer, the Swiss scientist. He was an elderly man with a straggly, white beard and he told us he had suffered from insomnia for a number of years and the only solution he had found to the problem was to get up and go for short walks. This explained why he had been up and about and I, certainly, believed him. When asked if he had spotted anybody else while on his travels, he produced an interesting revelation.

'I heard somebody in the bar and found a cleaner in there emptying the dishwasher. He very kindly made me a cup of camomile tea and while I was drinking it, I'm sure somebody came past and went out of the French windows – they were wide open – but because I was facing the bar, I didn't manage to turn around in time to see who it was.'

'And what time was that, please?'

'The clock behind the bar said just after two o'clock.'

'And after that, you went back to your room?'

'Yes, I did, and I'm pleased to say that I managed to get a reasonable night's sleep.'

When he left the room, I saw Bruno draw a line through Doctor Meyer's name.

'I think we can rule him out of our enquiries.' He checked his notepad again. 'I have a feeling the next names on the list are going to be the interesting ones.'

I nodded in agreement. 'Definitely.'

13

SUNDAY MORNING

Before the next interviewee could be shown in, one of the police officers from outside arrived with a message for Bruno. 'The local mayor's just arrived with a couple of his councillors and he wants to talk to you.'

Bruno looked across at me and raised his eyebrows. 'The mayor?' He returned his attention to the police officer. 'Well, do ask them to come in.'

The mayor was quite something. He was so tall, his head almost brushed the door frame and even Oscar looked up in awe as this giant of a man came in. He was wearing a formal, dark suit and his official sash of office, emblazoned with the green, white and red of the Italian flag. The most striking feature of his face was a magnificent handlebar moustache that almost reached his ears. One thing was for certain: no witness would have had trouble picking him out of an ID parade. Behind him came two other people: a diminutive woman probably in her sixties or even seventies, and behind her, none other than Giorgio Carbonaro from the winery. Bruno stood up and shook hands with all three of them.

'Good morning, Mr Mayor. How can I help?'

'Good morning, Inspector.' The Mayor of Pontenuovo had one of those gravelly voices that sound as if they gargle with razor blades. He drew himself up even taller and caught hold of his lapels in both hands and expanded his massive chest with no little pomp. The buttons of his shirt protested at the pressure and I instinctively turned my head. If they started popping, they could put an eye out. Unaware of the stress to which he was submitting his clothing, the mayor launched into his speech. 'It's about the wolves. We need to do something about them. The situation is unsustainable and something must be done.' I saw him eye the tabletop and could tell he was dying to bang his fist on it, but he managed to suppress the instinct.

'What wolves?' Bruno affected an air of incomprehension.

'The wolves that killed that poor man, of course.' The mayor was now in full flow and I saw the lady behind him nodding approvingly. In fairness, Giorgio Carbonaro who, thanks to me, knew otherwise, remained impassive.

Bruno did a wonderful job of keeping his expression amicable and his tone level. 'You're referring to the murder of a scientist here on Friday night, I imagine. Let me assure you that wolves were in no way involved, although an attempt was made by the killer to try to lay the blame on them.'

'That's not what I've heard.' The mayor's voice went up an octave and I saw Oscar raise his head again with an expression on his face indicating that he resented being woken from what had probably been an enjoyable dream about squirrels.

Bruno's expression hardened. 'I don't know what you've heard, Mr Mayor, but you can take it from me that this is a murder investigation which has nothing to do with wolves, and that's official.' His tone became uncompromising. 'But I'm pleased that you've come. There's been a suggestion that the murderer might be somebody from around here, deliberately trying to engineer a quite unjustified cull of an endangered species.' He allowed a bit more menace to enter his voice. 'It's possible that you may even have a murderer within your local community. We're currently carrying out our investigations here at the hotel, but we may well broaden our enquiries to include Pontenuovo, and you'll be the first to hear if we decide to interview you or any of your fellow citizens.'

I was impressed. This wasn't the first time I'd come across self-important politicians, both at a local and at a national level, and I'd learnt that the only way to deal with them was to fight fire with fire – and hope they didn't play golf with the chief constable. Bruno couldn't have done better. The three visitors eyed each other apprehensively and maybe even suspiciously, and their initial air of antagonism disappeared at a stroke.

Bruno pressed home his advantage. 'Thank you for taking the time to come and see me, Mr Mayor, but I'm afraid now I really must continue with this murder investigation. For the avoidance of any doubt, let me repeat that this is a *murder* investigation, which has nothing, repeat nothing, to do with anything with four legs.'

With impeccable timing, Oscar, who was no doubt getting fed up with the constant interruptions to his beauty sleep, produced one of his trademark part-whine, part-howl, part-yawn noises and I was delighted to see all three of our visitors jump apprehensively. After another round of handshakes and muted farewells, our three guests left and, once the door had closed behind them, I looked across at the inspector and gave him a broad grin.

'*Complimenti,* Bruno!'

He smiled back. 'That should keep them off our backs. Now, let's get on with the investigation.'

The next person to be interviewed was Massimo Santini, but we got nothing more out of him. Yes, he had known the victim and no, he would never dream of killing anybody. Besides, he had been in his room on his own all night and hadn't gone out. We queried whether somebody had knocked at his door in the middle of the night, resulting in an argument, but he shook his head and disclaimed all knowledge of it. I still didn't completely trust him but it was really only another of my old copper's hunches. I couldn't put my finger on it, but something about him didn't ring true.

He was followed by Freja Blomqvist. Given that she and I knew each other – albeit fairly superficially – I let Bruno do all the questioning and just acted as interpreter. It felt a little bit strange to be interviewing a fellow author as a potential suspect in a murder case but the fact remained that she had been far from convincing about her relations with the victim. At first she denied having had a relationship with Diamantis but, after Bruno had reminded her in no uncertain terms that this was a murder investigation and she was expected to tell the complete truth, she finally admitted it. Her answer reminded me of the one I had received from Monica Fowler the previous day.

'I've known him on and off for three or four years and we occasionally met up and had fun together. He was a very desirable man. From the very first moment I saw him, I couldn't take my eyes off him. I used to run into him from time to time at conferences and other professional meetings like this symposium, but I could hardly describe it as a relationship.' She looked across at me and grinned. 'It was just sex.'

Fortunately, I was not required to respond to this as Bruno continued. 'Would you say you were in love with him?'

She laughed. 'Of course not, it was a purely physical thing. There's no way I could fall in love with somebody for whom infidelity was more a challenge than a constraint. Besides, I love my husband.'

This came as a surprise and I couldn't help butting in. 'You're married?'

She nodded. 'Yes, I've been married for eleven years now.'

'Happily married?'

'Very happily married, thank you.' She couldn't have missed the disbelief on both our faces. 'We all have our little weaknesses. Mine is tall, dark, handsome men.' She batted her eyelids at me. 'Men like you, Inspector Dan.'

An immediate response didn't present itself to me. As far as I was concerned, the only handsome, dark-haired male in my household was Oscar. Being a suspicious old so-and-so, my immediate reaction was that she was deliberately trying to ingratiate herself with me because she had something to hide. Like murder, for example? I was saved from having to reply by Bruno continuing the questioning, and I reverted to interpreter status.

'And have you had a sexual relationship with any of the other delegates here at this symposium?'

She shook her head. 'No, Nico was the only one.'

'What about Massimo Santini? We've been told that he had his eye on you.'

'I've noticed.' Her tone was dry. 'He does make it a bit obvious, but it doesn't matter because I'm not interested in him. No, like I told you, Nico was the one and only.

Bruno wasn't letting it go. 'What about your Czech friend, Doctor Havel?'

She laughed again. 'Red hair and a beard? You must be joking, Inspector. Besides, Pavel's happily married with three children back in Prague. No, we're just friends, good friends, but nothing more.'

'Were you with Doctor Diamantis on Friday night?'

A moment of hesitation. 'No, he wasn't available.'

'What does that mean?'

'He told me he had to work.'

'And did you believe him?'

'I know he was a very busy man.' But she didn't sound convinced and neither was I.

Once she had left, Bruno and I stopped for a short break and Officer Gori appeared with two cups of coffee. After thanking him, I shot a question at him. He was a bright boy and I was interested to give him a chance to tell us what he thought.

'Any hunches as to the identity of the murderer yet, Gori?'

'Not really.' He lowered his voice even though the door was closed. 'But the guy with the beard who's next on your list looks as though he'd happily murder the sergeant and me.' He shook his head. 'A bit too full of himself if you ask me.'

I glanced across at Bruno. 'That must be Thomas Cartwright. It sounds as though Gori's opinion of him is similar to mine. Let's see what you think.'

It's fair to say that Thomas Cartwright didn't distinguish himself in the interview that followed. He was irascible, difficult, and ridiculously full of himself. Yes, I reckoned Gori had got him dead to rights. But, his prickly personality aside, he didn't say anything to make either of us suspect him of murder, even though we pressed him on the argument he had had with the victim out on the terrace on Friday afternoon. He simply told us it had been a professional scientific matter that mere policemen like us wouldn't understand. Of course he had spent that night in his own bed. Where else? As for a noisy altercation outside his room, he hadn't heard a thing. When he left the room, we were both pleased to see him go, but he hadn't advanced our inquiries in any way.

He was followed by Pavel Havel and neither of us felt that he was our man. He was clearly very nervous but murder inquiries can have that effect on people. We showed him the wooden wolf caller that Oscar had found. His reaction was considerable curiosity but absolutely no guilt. When asked about his relationship with Freja, he looked bewildered that we might suspect him of harbouring carnal intentions towards her and just shook his head blankly.

This left us with the couple from Manchester. First to come in was Monica Fowler, whose red-rimmed eyes attested to her grief. She repeated what she had told me the previous afternoon, namely that she had been head over heels in love with Diamantis but had not been with him on the night of the murder. When queried why this had been, she replied rather unconvincingly that she had had a headache. Having a headache as far as my ex-wife was concerned had often been shorthand for being seriously pissed off with me. I wondered whether the Greek might have done something that night to annoy the woman who claimed to have loved him. After all, Anna and I had seen him canoodling with a number of other women. Maybe he had hooked up with a different partner instead of her? We pressed her a few times about her open marriage and her husband before, finally, Bruno asked her outright whether she thought her husband might have killed Diamantis out of jealousy. Her answer was immediate and uncompromising, but what she said afterwards was interesting.

'Absolutely not. There's no way Peter could ever kill anybody. But I'm surprised if he told you he didn't have an alibi. I'm quite sure he had company that night.'

'Who do you think he was with?'

'You'll have to ask him that.'

We did.

It took a while but finally, he caved in and his answer surprised us. 'I still feel this is an outrageous invasion of my privacy but, if you absolutely have to know, I spent the night with Thomas.'

Suddenly the open-marriage thing became more understandable. As my old super used to say in a rare canine metaphor, it appeared that Professor Peter Fowler preferred his Pal to his Lassie. After quizzing and dismissing Fowler, Bruno took considerable pleasure in summoning Thomas Cartwright once again and extracting confirmation from him that he had indeed been with Peter Fowler, telling him he might well be charged with impeding a murder investigation and wasting police time. It was a far less cocky and a more chastened Thomas who left the room after that dressing-down. After the door closed behind him, Bruno dropped his pen down on top of his pad and looked across at me.

'Feel like a breath of fresh air?'

I had known for some time that Oscar's comprehension skills in both English and Italian encompassed the words for walks and food, but somehow he must have understood Bruno perfectly as he immediately jumped to his feet and headed for the door. We followed.

Outside in the garden, the air was quite warm although the sky was becoming increasingly overcast. We walked around to the far side of the hotel where the formal gardens finished and a small olive grove began. While Oscar did his best to mark every single tree we passed, Bruno referred me to the morning's interviews.

'Well, who's your money on?'

'I'm still trying to make up my mind *why* Diamantis was killed. Was it out of jealousy or was he maybe the target of an attempt by anti-wolf activists to bring about the end of the animals' protected status by faking an assault? The hotel gardener, the farmer last night and the mayor today are probably representative of a large proportion of the farming community.'

'Yes, okay, but murder?' Bruno sounded sceptical. 'It's one thing for protesters to hold rallies or glue themselves to bridges, but to resort to murder? Sounds pretty crazy to me.'

'I know what you mean but I include it as a possibility, just like there's a vague possibility that Diamantis was being targeted by the fossil fuels industry or was being trolled by some loony on social media.' I had already told Bruno that my cursory look at the victim's social media accounts had revealed nothing apart from that one photo where Freja had been hanging onto Diamantis most affectionately.

Bruno nodded in agreement. 'I think we can agree that the more likely answer is that it was a crime of passion. Everybody acknowledges that he had a reputation as a serial womaniser, so it's probable that he was either killed by a disappointed or jilted lover or by somebody who felt Diamantis had robbed him of the woman he loved. Agreed?'

I was quick to agree. 'Definitely, and on that basis, I think we can eliminate Peter Fowler and Thomas Cartwright on the grounds of their sexuality – besides, they both now have alibis – and I would be amazed if Hans Meyer had anything to do with it. I think we can also eliminate the Irishman, Greengrass, as he had other fish to fry and, by the same token, I think we can eliminate the two Spanish ladies, his frying companions.' I was counting the names off on my list. 'Juliette, Ingrid and Carla didn't strike me as interested enough in Diamantis to consider killing him, and I think Havel the Czech's also in the clear.'

Bruno nodded. 'I completely agree as far as all of these are concerned. What about the others?'

I paused to pick up a stick that my dog had deposited at my feet. We both knew what I had to do with it, and so I slung it as far down the track ahead of us as possible and watched him run off after it. 'There's something about that Roman guy, Santini, that doesn't quite sit right with me, but I can't think of any firm motive he might have had for murder. Professional jealousy seems to be out of the question as he and Diamantis had completely different fields of interest. Maybe jealousy of a more intimate kind, given that it sounds as though he had the hots for Freja and maybe Monica Fowler as well. If the victim had been involved with either of them, maybe Santini was trying to eliminate a rival, but it's going to be hard to prove.'

Bruno grunted in agreement and I carried on.

'As far as I can see, we have three prime suspects: Monica Fowler, Freja Blomqvist and Massimo Santini. Both women were in a relationship with the victim, although they claim they weren't with him that night, but there's no proof either way. Maybe one of them killed him because they suspected him of hooking up with another woman. Alternatively, there's Santini, who might have murdered Diamantis because the Greek had stolen his woman or some such – but who that woman might be remains a mystery.' I caught his eye. 'But it's flimsy to say the least.'

At that moment, Gori came running up the track after us with the list of names written by the various interviewees and we stopped while I studied them closely. At my bidding, he had also made a surreptitious note of whether they had been left- or right-handed. The results were interesting, if inconclusive. Exactly half of the fourteen were left-handed and four of these were women: Pilar Gomez, Carla Vespucci, Freja Blomqvist and Monica Fowler. The other three left-handers were Peter Fowler, Pavel Havel and Massimo Santini. As for similarities in the handwriting, without Mrs Connelly, I was unable to tell.

Bruno and I looked at each other and I shrugged my shoulders. 'Doesn't help a lot, does it?'

'It was worth a try.'

He thanked Gori and sent him back into the hotel while Bruno and I carried on with our walk. Bruno scanned his notebook as we made our way up the track. 'I'm not sure how much the handwriting helps but at least this morning, we've been able to pare the list down a bit. For me, the Fowler woman is top of the list, followed by Blomqvist and Santini. There's also potentially Peter Fowler, but

he now has an alibi, albeit furnished by his homosexual lover.
There's still the possibility, however unlikely, that the murderer
came from outside the scientific community for whatever reason,
but the fact remains that only a handful of the other guests at the
hotel have an alibi for that night and it would appear that there was
a good bit of bed-swapping going on. It strikes me that this symposium hasn't just been about science.' He grinned at me.

I grinned back at him. 'Maybe one of them should write a
scholarly paper on their extra-curricular activities – there appears
to have been no shortage of those.'

14

SUNDAY AFTERNOON

Anna and I met up with Virgilio and Lina just before midday and travelled to Siena in my car with Oscar in the back. As we left, two coaches came up the drive towards us, no doubt here to collect the delegates and transfer them to Siena for their lunch and their tour of the historic city. During the twenty-minute journey, Virgilio and his wife didn't say a lot but they were looking reasonably happy. I was keeping my fingers crossed for them. I could tell that Virgilio was dying to find out how the investigation was going but he managed to summon the self-control not to mention it and I had already agreed with Anna that anything to do with police work was taboo for today.

Oscar is a very sociable dog. So sociable, in fact, that he sometimes sticks his nose where he shouldn't. The good news today was that Siena in early April, while busy, was far less crowded than it would be in the summer months, and the people were mostly wearing long trousers. Oscar has a particular liking for ladies in short shorts but, understandably, not everybody likes having a cold Labrador nose goosing them as they go about their business. So today was less stressful than it would have been in high summer for me hanging onto the end of his lead, though I knew that having him with us was going to cramp my style as far as going into historic buildings was concerned. But that was a problem for the afternoon. Right now, we were having lunch and Virgilio had kindly picked a restaurant where dogs were welcome.

The restaurant he had chosen was tucked away in a narrow street lined with medieval houses roughly halfway between the iconic Piazza del Campo and the duomo. It was also barely a hundred metres from the *questura*, the police station where Bruno worked. I rather suspected that this might not be a coincidence, but I didn't comment and followed him in through the door. This was set in a fairly bland façade built of the same rose-pink, medieval bricks from which much of the rest of the city is made and we were ushered down a flight of brick steps into what had clearly once been a vast cellar. The vaulted ceiling was bare brick, and a huge fireplace at the far end would no doubt provide welcome warmth on cold, winter nights. Wooden shelves around the walls were laden with bottles of wine, not surprisingly most of them different varieties of Chianti. It was intimate, it was ancient, it was atmospheric, and it just screamed Tuscany. I had a feeling we were going to eat well here.

My confidence proved to be well founded.

It was just as well that I was hungry. The first thing to arrive on our table was a massive wooden platter loaded with hand-carved ham and salami, slices of three or four different types of pecorino cheese, ranging from fresh and soft to over a year old and crunchy and, of course, the ubiquitous crostini or bruschetta. Today these were a mixture. There were simple toasted chunks of Tuscan unsalted bread rubbed with garlic and drizzled with thick olive oil and along with these were the other traditional types of bruschetta, some topped with chopped tomatoes in olive oil, some with chicken liver pate, and some topped with slices of roast red peppers, still hot from the oven.

As we ate our antipasti, we chatted – still studiously avoiding anything police-related – and Anna launched into her role as unpaid tour guide, drawing on her background in medieval history. She told us how back in the thirteen hundreds, Siena had been one of the most populous cities in Europe and a power to rival its now better-known neighbour, Florence, and even Rome itself. So much of the wonderful ancient architecture we would be visiting this afternoon had been built at that time, but Siena's rise to power had been dealt a quite literally mortal blow in 1348 with the arrival of the plague, the Black Death, which is believed to have killed as much as a third of the city's population, reducing the city to poverty and killing off so many of the talented artists and stonemasons.

Thought of death got me thinking once again about the murder of Diamantis. Hopefully one set of the fingerprints taken this morning would match with those found on the broken glass of the murder weapon. If that was the case, we would almost certainly have our perpetrator. I say 'almost certainly' because there still remained the possibility that Diamantis's killer had deliberately planted broken glass from a bottle recently touched by one of the other symposium participants in order to shift suspicion onto them, but I was keeping an open mind for now. Over the years, I had learnt never to discount any feasible hypothesis until proved otherwise. The fact was that if it turned out to be impossible to find a match, we would be left with precious little to go on.

The only other concrete clue we had was the crumpled note found in the victim's room, which had not yet revealed any readily identifiable prints on it. I found myself thinking yet again about the little drawing of a heart with an arrow through it in place of a signature. No doubt Diamantis would have assumed that he knew the identity of the writer, and the fact that he had gone outside also indicated that he had been willing and maybe happy to meet up. Given that we had ample proof that he had been a heterosexual, it seemed logical to assume that this person must have been a woman. Although, I reminded myself, there was always the chance that it had been written by a man pretending to be a woman, whoever that might have been.

Anna and Lina protested weakly that they didn't want pasta before the main course, which was going to be roast wild boar, but the restaurateur insisted on giving everybody a taste of his special *gnudi*. These weird green gnocchi were completely new to me, and Virgilio explained that they were made using spinach and ricotta, but with semolina instead of potato. The little dumplings were about the size of Brussels sprouts and were tasty but immensely filling, so I made sure I didn't eat too many of them. Anna took only two – I counted them – and pronounced them excellent. Virgilio, I noticed, took a liberal helping and finished the lot. Marital problems often seem to increase the appetite. Far too many takeaways and fish and chips in the final months of my unhappy marriage had been responsible for me putting on quite a few unwanted pounds. I cast an affectionate glance at Oscar stretched out at my feet. Getting him had not only provided me with an excellent companion, but all the long walks had certainly been good for my waistline.

The roast wild boar was exquisite; the meat was so tender it just fell apart, and the little roast potatoes flavoured with rosemary that accompanied it were delightful. By the time I had finished my plate, I was surreptitiously reaching down to undo the top button on my jeans. Tuscan food certainly provides no shortage of calories and I almost said no to the exquisite crème brûlée... I did say 'almost'.

After lunch, Anna led me on a tour of the *centro storico*, steadfastly refusing to let the other two come with us, telling them they needed a bit of quality time by themselves. To be honest, I was delighted to have a bit of quality time with Anna all to myself. We had been going out now for about six months and things had been going very well between us, and it was more than pleasant to be able to stroll around this beautiful city with her by my side while she demonstrated her encyclopaedic knowledge of medieval history. From time to time, we spotted individuals or small groups of scientists from the symposium, but they didn't bother us and we didn't bother them.

I had received an email a couple of days earlier from my journalist friend, Jess, giving me the good news that she had managed to get her article about a certain former Metropolitan-police-inspector-turned-author into *The Sunday Times*, no less. When I spotted a newsagent with foreign newspapers displayed on a rack outside, I checked to see if they had a copy, but papers from the UK were all one day old. I would have to wait. Hopefully, she hadn't been too critical of the book – assuming she had had time to read it – and I was optimistic that this would help with sales. When I had told Suzanne at my publishers, she had sounded very enthusiastic, so I was hoping for the best.

Our walk led us inevitably to Piazza del Campo, the beating heart of the town. This fan-shaped piazza paved with red bricks is the site of the famous *palio* horse races that take place every summer. Some time, I knew I would have to come and see the *palio* for myself but, for now, it was most pleasant to wander around in the spring sunshine not being hemmed in on all sides by spectators or jostled by hordes of tourists. The piazza itself slopes downwards towards the Palazzo Pubblico and the Torre del Mangia, a slim, red-brick tower rising over a hundred metres to its marble-clad top where energetic visitors can climb the four hundred steps so as to enjoy a fantastic view of the city. I've never been a great one for heights and so I happily passed on the offer to climb it. I had little doubt that if I had been forced to go up to the top, I would definitely not have dared to look back down.

Anna was such a knowledgeable local guide that she knew a few less-well-known but outstandingly beautiful places, prime amongst which was the *Facciatone*. Built at the rear of the duomo, a few hundred yards from the Piazza del Campo, this unique and massive structure made of red brick and black and white marble had been intended to become part of what would have been the biggest religious building in Europe way back in the fourteenth century. This had been when the city was at the height of its power and wealth but, of course, the plague had put paid to that. The translation of the name is the 'big façade' and to the modern eye, it is just a huge unfinished wall, almost as high as the cathedral, complete with arched window openings bereft of glass, standing on its own, looking rather forlorn. I could see tiny figures moving about high above on the open terraces at the top but, once again, I had absolutely no intention of joining them.

After a full afternoon of sightseeing, I was sitting outside the duomo just after half past five, taking a well-earned rest with Oscar sprawled at my feet while Anna went in to check out a statue that interested her when my phone started ringing. It was Bruno, and he had big news.

'We have a match. We have our killer. Want to take a guess who it is?'

I had been mulling over that same question on and off all afternoon and each time had whittled it down to our three possibles. I took a chance and opted for the man, rather than either of the two women. 'I'm going to say Massimo Santini. There's just something about him that didn't stack up. Any good?'

'*Bravissimo*, Dan. Dead right. Forensics managed to get a good set of prints and the match is unequivocal. We've got him. The scientists are all supposed to be going back to their coaches in the next twenty minutes or so, and I'll be waiting there with my men to arrest him. If you feel like coming along, please do. If you see Virgilio, do tell him as well, won't you?'

Although I had called it, there was still a lingering doubt at the back of my mind that Santini might have been framed, but when Anna came out of the cathedral and I gave her the good news, I didn't mention my reservations. She sounded relieved, as I was sure the other attendees would be when they heard. She declined the invitation to come along to the coaches to witness the arrest, but she happily took a seat outside a nearby café with Oscar to look after her – and beg for biscuits – while I hurried through the narrow streets to see for myself. I toyed with the idea of calling Virgilio with the news but remembered my resolve to avoid mention of police work and decided that could wait until we met up as agreed back at the car.

The two coaches were waiting at the pick-up point just outside the medieval centre and were already well over half full. Uniformed officers were checking off names on clipboards as the delegates arrived so that nobody would be left behind. I spotted Bruno and his sergeant waiting expectantly and I went across to wait with them. It's always satisfying to finally catch a killer and I knew it was going to be doubly satisfying to see the perpetrator of such a gory murder apprehended. Bruno gave me a little wave when he saw me.

'*Ciao*, Dan, I'm looking forward to this. Santini hasn't returned yet but hopefully he'll be back any moment.' He didn't quite rub his palms together with glee as Virgilio would have done, but there was no mistaking the delight on his face. 'Just thirty-six hours to solve a murder is pretty good going, don't you think?'

'Definitely. I'm sorry Virgilio isn't here to see it as well.'

He lowered his voice and glanced around. 'How are things

between him and Lina Would I be right in thinking that they've been having problems? They've always struck me as the perfect couple.'

I nodded. 'Me too. You're right, things aren't too good for them at the moment. We both know it isn't easy being married to a cop. My own marriage ended in disaster for that very reason. What about you? Are you married?'

He shook his head. 'Sorry to hear that. No, I've been in a couple of long-term relationships, but neither of them lasted. You know how it is... It's the job.'

We carried on chatting as we watched the last few scientists return to the coaches, but I still hadn't been able to spot Santini. My excitement started to wane and I began to face the prospect that our perpetrator might have taken advantage of his few hours of freedom here in Siena to make a run for it. The same thoughts must have been going through Bruno's head as he rattled off instructions to his sergeant to get his men to do a headcount and double-check every name just in case the Roman had slipped on board one of the buses without being recorded. We gave it another fifteen minutes for the last few stragglers to return, but there was still no sign of Santini. Finally, we had to accept the inevitable conclusion. The bird had flown but there was no point crying over spilt milk.

Bruno sent the coaches on their way back to the hotel and was just issuing orders to his men to organise a full-scale manhunt, starting with railway stations and airports, when his sergeant took a phone call and immediately interrupted the inspector.

'A body's been found, sir. It's Santini.' My ears pricked up. What did this mean? Had he killed himself or was this another murder?

Bruno directed all his attention at the sergeant. 'Santini's dead? Where and how?'

'It's looking like suicide. They say it looks like he threw himself off the *Facciatone*.'

'Suicide!' Bruno glanced across at me. 'Might he have realised we were on to him or was he suddenly overcome with remorse?'

'Are we sure it was suicide?' I've often been accused of being a bit too cynical and not taking things at face value, but it was a possibility that couldn't be ignored. 'What if he was pushed? What if there's another murderer at the symposium? Or what if the two scientists were murdered by person or persons unknown from outside the group?'

Bruno nodded in agreement. 'Anything's possible. I think we need to get over to the *Facciatone* as soon as possible. You coming, Dan?'

I glanced at my watch. It was ten to six and I had arranged to meet the others back at the car at six o'clock. Although my natural instincts were for me to go with him, Bruno wasn't going to need my help with translating and I had to remind myself that this wasn't my murder investigation, after all, so I shook my head – although it went against the grain. 'Unless you need me, I'll head back to the hotel. If you want me to help with more interviews, just shout. All right with you?'

'Of course. Thanks a lot for all your help so far.' He gave a frustrated snort. 'I hope it was suicide or we're going to be right back at square one all over again.'

I shared his frustration. Somehow it had all been too easy and now, suddenly, it looked as though our house of cards might have come tumbling down.

15

SUNDAY EVENING

In spite of my promise to avoid talking shop, I felt I had to tell the others what I had just learnt, and the mood in the car on the way back to the hotel was subdued as a result. Even Oscar just lay down with a thud and closed his eyes, but he was probably tired after his long walk around the *centro storico*. When we got back to the hotel, we met the two coaches coming back along the drive towards us again after unloading the remaining scientists. Was there a second killer among them?

What if it hadn't been suicide? I couldn't help wondering if Santini's motive for killing Diamantis might not have been out of jealousy at all. Maybe there were more sinister forces at work here. These were all pretty eminent scientists, after all. Might there be industrial or state espionage involved, by any chance? The finger-print evidence against the Roman was damning, but could it have been fabricated so as to draw suspicion away from the real killer?

The fact was that the broken bottle and the wolf caller had been left suspiciously close to the open French windows of the hotel. The assumption was that they had been dropped in a panic by Santini as he rushed away from the scene of the crime, but maybe they had been deliberately put there, where they would easily be found. But, if somebody had done this to frame Santini, why go to all the trouble of incriminating him only to then kill him the next day? I was still pondering this when I drew up in the car park and I was mildly surprised to hear Lina make a suggestion from the back seat.

'Dan, why don't you and Virgilio go and have a beer? I'm going upstairs to take a bath.'

Anna immediately added weight to the suggestion. 'I think I'm going to do exactly the same thing. Why don't you two men go and talk about murder? Get it out of your systems before dinner.'

I reached over and gave her hand a squeeze. She really did know me so well by now. 'Well, if you're sure, I must admit that a beer sounds good. Virgilio, you coming?'

By now, the sky was almost completely overcast, but it was still warm enough for the two of us to sit down on the terrace outside the bar with the Labrador at our feet. As ever, Oscar was looking hungry – in spite of having been given a huge piece of prime steak left over by one of the lunchtime diners who had been unable to finish it. I made sure we were far enough away from any inquisitive ears as I took Virgilio through what I had heard from Bruno in more detail and he shook his head helplessly.

'It has to be suicide, surely. I reckon Santini must be the person who murdered Diamantis and he took his own life because he couldn't handle the guilt, don't you agree?' He knew me well enough by now to hold up his hand before I butted in. 'Yes, I know the Greek might have been murdered by somebody else, who then for some reason tried to incriminate Santini by getting hold of a bottle with his prints on it and leaving it for us to find. But if so, why go to all that trouble and then kill him?'

I had to agree. 'Yes, I've been through all that in my head as well, and suicide would be the obvious answer, but of course it remains to be seen whether he did jump or whether he was pushed.'

We were interrupted by a visitor. I glanced up to see Peter Fowler coming along the terrace towards us. He was looking furtive and I wondered what he might have to say for himself.

'Good evening, gentlemen. There's something I need to tell you but I've been agonising over it ever since we spoke this morning. I'm afraid I wasn't completely frank and open with you. I should have told you before. The thing is that on Friday night, I saw somebody.'

Although I was sure that Virgilio had understood, I answered, seeing as I had interviewed him this morning. 'Who did you see and when exactly did you see them, Professor Fowler?'

'It was just before two o'clock in the morning.' He was looking decidedly sheepish. 'The thing is, like I say, I didn't tell you the whole truth before. I told you that I spent the night with Thomas but in fact he and I got into a blazing row and I stormed off and left in the middle of the night.'

'And that was around two o'clock in the morning? And did your argument spill out into the corridor?' That would explain what Doctor Albese had said about having heard an argument outside his door. Seeing Fowler nod, I asked the other question again. 'So who did you see and where?'

He looked around nervously yet again and lowered his voice even more. 'Massimo Santini. I saw him going down the back stairs. I don't think he saw me and I'd be really grateful if you wouldn't make public that I've told you I saw him. He and I aren't exactly friends, and if he thinks I'm trying to get him into trouble, things could get rather awkward.'

I exchanged glances with Virgilio and saw him give the slightest shake of the head. I knew what he meant – I was thinking the same thing myself. There was no need to advertise the fact that

Santini was dead until we had all the facts. I answered honestly. 'I can promise you that Doctor Santini won't know that you told us this. Tell me, Professor Fowler, why is it that you and he don't get on?'

Again the furtive glance over his shoulder. 'Monica, my wife, has been having an affair with Santini for a year or more although, for all I know, that might now be over. Thomas told me he'd heard that she'd been having an affair with Diamantis more recently, and from her reaction to his death, I imagine that's probably true. Whether she was carrying on with one or the other of them honestly doesn't bother me. We live separate lives so we're both free to be with whoever we like. The thing is, Santini knows that I know about his relationship with her, and I suppose deep down, he's afraid I might choose to cause a scandal for him by making their affair public. It means that relations between me and him have always been strained as a result.'

Virgilio didn't waste any time, making sure he stuck with the present tense when referring to Santini. 'And you really don't resent him sleeping with your wife?'

'No, like I told you, that's her business, not mine.'

I had a thought. 'Your argument with Thomas in the middle of the night, what was that about?'

'It was a work thing. It was a stupid argument, but then most late-night arguments are, aren't they? Basically, I told him he had to come clean and admit that he'd copied some elements of Nikolaos's research and apologise to him and to the scientific community. He swore at me and refused to accept what I said. He isn't the sort of person who likes criticism and he was really furious.'

Furious enough to go out and kill the man whose work he was alleged to have copied? I tried another tack. 'Presumably you and Thomas agreed in advance to say that you'd been together all night. Whose idea was that?'

'Um, Thomas's I think.'

'And why do you think he might have suggested that?'

There was a pause. 'I suppose, once we'd been told about the murder, he was concerned that the fact that I was walking about in the middle of the night might have made me a suspect.'

'So you think he suggested it so as to protect you?'

Fowler nodded.

'You don't think it might have been to protect himself?'

'Protect himself? You surely don't think he had anything to do with Diamantis's death.' Fowler looked aghast. 'He'd never do anything like that, I promise you.'

Virgilio and I exchanged glances before he asked a final question. 'Is there anything else you haven't told us, Professor Fowler? Think very carefully.'

He shook his head and we let him go. As he disappeared back into the bar again, I looked across at Virgilio. 'Do we believe him when he says Diamantis's and Santini's affairs with his wife didn't bother him? What if Fowler wasn't as untroubled by her carryings-on as he would like us to think? Maybe he killed both of the men who were supposedly her sexual partners? That's a pretty clear motive. Alternatively, could it be that a third party killed Diamantis, and then Fowler took advantage of the confusion caused by that murder to settle accounts with Santini, his wife's other lover? Mind you, seeing as this now means that Thomas Cartwright no longer has an alibi for Friday night, what if *he* had worked himself up into such a rage that he went out and murdered Diamantis after all? But that doesn't help us find Santini's murderer – if indeed it was murder.'

Before Virgilio could respond, my phone started ringing. It was Bruno.

'It looks like it was suicide.' I could hear the relief in his voice. 'Santini's body was found stuck between the roofs of two of the surrounding houses. There's no way of knowing how high up he was when he jumped, but the body was a hell of a mess. Nobody saw or heard him fall so it's hard to establish the exact time of death. What was left of him was spotted by a sharp-eyed Swiss tourist at just before five, and it took half an hour for the emergency services to get up to him and to discover his ID. They've only just retrieved the body now. The pathologist will do a full autopsy but her first impression, like mine, was that there were no signs of a struggle or any injuries other than those to be expected after a catastrophic fall. So, hopefully, everybody can sleep well tonight knowing that we got the right man. Santini killed Diamantis in order to remove his rival for Monica Fowler's affections. He subsequently regretted his actions and committed suicide, helpfully saving us the trouble of having to charge him and try him.'

After telling Bruno what we had just heard from Peter Fowler, which added even further confirmation to the likelihood that Santini had indeed killed the Greek, I relayed the good news about the apparent suicide to Virgilio and we drank to it. I enjoyed the cold beer but I still couldn't shift a feeling of something still not quite being right. But if there hadn't been any witnesses to Santini's death and there were no signs of a struggle, then presumably we would have to accept the fact that it had been suicide brought on by a guilty conscience and that was that.

After the news had sunk in, I turned the conversation to relations between Virgilio and his wife and he shrugged his shoulders.

'We've had a couple of good long talks and I understand what's going through her head. The fact is that Lina's worried for me, worried that something might happen to me. The kids have grown up and left home and she's on her own much of the time and she finds herself worrying more and more. To be honest, I think half the trouble is that she's bored. When the kids were at home, they kept her occupied and she had less time to worry or she worried about them. Now that's all been transferred to worry about me.'

'Any thoughts on how you can improve matters?'

He shrugged again. 'Short of finding myself another job, it's hard to come up with a solution.'

'What about Lina getting herself a job? If she could find something that interests her and gets her mixing with people, that would probably go a long way, wouldn't it?'

'That's what Anna said to her, but the problem is, what sort of job?'

* * *

Dinner that evening was another open buffet and, needless to say, none of us felt particularly hungry after our massive lunch – apart from my four-legged friend, who was always hungry, of course, and he happily crunched his way through a whole pack of grissini. At least Lina was sounding a bit more upbeat this evening and it was an enjoyable meal for the four of us. Towards the end, as I was standing by the dessert table trying to make up my mind whether a panna cotta with blackberry coulis would finally explode the waistband of my jeans, I felt a tap on my arm. I turned to see the earnest face of Carla Vespucci, the slug specialist, and she had a question for me.

'I'm sorry to bother you but I've been looking for Massimo... Massimo Santini, and I can't see him anywhere.'

I decided to put on my gormless expression. I'm quite good at that and my ex-wife had often commented on it – but not in a good way. 'Maybe he's having a lie down.' I wondered if there was a special reason why she was looking for the Roman, so I decided it wouldn't hurt to throw a stone into the pond and see where the ripples led. After all, Professor Pelletier had said Carla might have been interested in Diamantis so, if she was in the market for a man, maybe she had also had an interest in Santini. 'Maybe he's disappeared off with a girlfriend?'

If I'd been hoping this would bring colour to her cheeks, I was to be disappointed. She just shook her head and carried on. 'I saw him in Siena, but I didn't get a chance to talk to him. Do you think he maybe missed the bus back to the hotel?'

'I've no idea. Are you looking for him about something special?'

She shook her head. 'No, it's a work thing and I was just wondering where he was, that's all. Thanks anyway.'

I wandered over to where Virgilio was helping himself to slabs of pecorino cheese and some really soft Gorgonzola dolce. I relayed the short conversation I had just had with Carla to him and he nodded pensively. 'Do we think she fancied Santini?'

'I really don't know. The French professor said she thought it was Diamantis that Carla liked but maybe she was wrong. To be honest, with those awful glasses and her schoolmarm hairstyle, I'm not sure how appealing she would have been to either of the two men.'

'There's no accounting for taste. By the way, this Gorgonzola is amazing.'

* * *

After dinner, Anna and I took Oscar for a walk. Tonight, the moon was completely obscured by thick cloud and there was already a hint of moisture in the air. It was very pleasant out here far away from air and light pollution and, even without the moonlight, once our eyes had acclimatised to the dark, we were able to find our way quite easily up the white gravel track. We chatted from time to time but mostly just walked in comfortable silence, enjoying each other's company and the peace and quiet.

However, just as we were approaching the copse where Oscar liked to forage for pine cones, the silence was broken by a long, protracted, mournful howl that set the hair on the back of my neck on end and brought my Labrador cowering to my side. This time there could be no doubt about it: this was the real McCoy and Oscar could tell. I felt Anna grip my arm tightly with both of her hands as she stopped dead and whispered in my ear.

'That wasn't far away. Do you think we're in any danger?'

I did my best to sound confident. 'For the last three days, everybody's been telling me that wolves won't attack humans, but it might be a different matter for Oscar.' I could feel him pressing against my legs and I'm sure he would have jumped into my arms if he could have done. 'I get the impression he feels the same way, so I think a strategic retreat might be the wisest option.'

When we got back to the hotel, we went into the bar for a coffee and I spotted Freja and Pavel sitting at a table on their own. As we walked past, I paused to tell them about the wolf howl and they both immediately looked animated. Doctor Havel jumped up, almost overturning his chair in his haste, closely followed by his Swedish counterpart.

'Can you tell us exactly where you heard it? I'd love to get a sighting of a wolf in the wild.'

As Freja got to her feet alongside him, I couldn't help noticing that her dress tonight was particularly revealing. I found my eyes drawn to a little gold pendant on a chain lurking deep down in the shadowy depths of her cleavage and a little warning bell started sounding in my head. Was that what I thought it was and, if so, what did it say about the innocence or guilt of my fellow author? I wondered if the femme fatale outfit was for the benefit of anybody special and, if so, who? Anna at my side must have noticed the direction of my eyes as I felt a proprietorial hand grip my arm and I hastened to return my attention to her.

'It was a really scary howl, wasn't it, Anna?'

'It certainly was; it terrified Oscar.' She glanced down to where my dog was leaning amorously against Freja's leg, now no longer looking in the least bit concerned. 'But he seems to have bounced back from his fright without a care in the world.'

Freja stroked his head and a dreamy expression appeared on his face. 'How exciting, do tell us where you heard the howl. It's so good to know that there are wolves close by. We must go and investigate, mustn't we, Pavel?' Although most unsuitably dressed for wolf hunting, Freja sounded enthusiastic at the prospect.

I carefully explained where we had been and the direction from which the howl had come, and they hurried out through the French windows. I almost told them to be careful but presumably they knew what they were doing. Rather them than me. That howl had somehow reached deep inside me and the fact that my normally carefree Labrador had been similarly affected just reinforced the primal nature of the sound. Whoever it was who first came up with the idea of werewolves knew what they were talking about.

Anna elbowed me in the ribs. 'Your Swedish friend does like her clothes – what little there is of them – doesn't she?'

'She certainly does. Tell me, did you by any chance look down her front?'

Anna gave me a suspicious look. 'No, I thought I would leave that to you, seeing as your eyes were out on stalks.'

'All in the line of duty, *carissima*. Unless I'm very much mistaken, I think I recognised the design of the pendant she was hiding down there. I might be wrong but it looked very much to me like a little heart with an arrow through it. Now, I wonder who might have given her that?'

16

MONDAY

Monday morning brought a not totally unexpected surprise. It had rained in the night and there were puddles on the tracks, but that wasn't the surprise. I was just coming back with Oscar from his pre-breakfast walk when a car pulled up. In it was Bruno and the surprise that wasn't a complete surprise came from him.

'Morning, Dan, bad news, I'm afraid. Santini – it wasn't suicide, it was murder after all. He was dead before he hit the roof.' My mind was already racing with the ramifications of this. I had been right to harbour doubts about the suicide but where did this leave the investigation?

Bruno went on to tell me that he had just received the pathologist's report, which indicated that she had located a minute wound to Santini's back just between the shoulder blades, directly in line with the heart. It had only been visible under the bright lights in the autopsy room and it had clearly been delivered with surgical precision as there had been almost no blood loss as a result. 'Donatella says it was inflicted with a slim blade no more than four or five millimetres wide and it pierced the right ventricle, stopping the heart almost instantly.'

'A stiletto? Could we be talking organised crime?' I remembered reading how Mafia assassins in the old days reputedly used to favour a stiletto as a weapon that was effective, silent and easy to hide. Whether they still used them these days, of course, was another matter. It sounded a bit too Hollywood for my liking.

He gave a frustrated sigh. 'God knows. Given that it happened in Siena and not at the hotel, then anybody could have done it, from the KGB to Father Christmas.'

'I still tend to think that it must have been one of the scientists from here. They were all walking around town yesterday afternoon, weren't they?' I thought back to my conversation with Virgilio the previous night. 'If we assume for a moment that it was somebody from here, the most likely motive is that Santini killed Diamantis and then somebody killed him in revenge.' I saw him nod his head but then felt I had better put the other theory, even if it didn't convince me. 'Alternatively, maybe the same person killed both Diamantis and Santini. But then why did they go to the trouble of trying to incriminate Santini, only to kill him the next day? It makes little sense. And, more to the point, what's the link between the two victims? Why were they killed? Who would have wanted both of them dead?'

'That's what I've been trying to find out. I've had people looking into the Greek's affairs – without finding anything untoward so far – and I'll do a full search of Santini's room along with a careful look into his background. And the same applies to our other main suspects for his murder: Freja Blomqvist, Monica and Peter Fowler and Thomas Cartwright. After what Fowler told you yesterday evening, we now know that none of them have independent alibis for Friday night when Diamantis was murdered. Fowler and Cartwright have provided alibis for each other up until two o'clock but, of course, they might have been in it together – for whatever reason. Freja and Monica claim to have slept alone but there's nobody to confirm that. Anybody else you think we should put on the list?'

'Nobody immediately springs to mind.' My mind was racing. 'I suppose we've still got to consider the possibility that they were both killed by somebody outside the symposium group, but I don't like it. My gut feeling is that Santini did indeed kill Diamantis and that his murder in Siena has to be linked with that, as a reprisal or revenge. If the murder of Diamantis was a crime of passion, then it's ever more likely that so was Santini's murder in Siena.'

He nodded his head. 'I quite agree. So what are we saying? Santini kills Diamantis because the Greek was involved with a woman that Santini loved, or at least lusted over – Monica Fowler presumably. Santini is then killed in revenge but who by? The same woman who was in love with Diamantis or another one? Or maybe Santini killed Diamantis on the instructions of a woman who had a grudge against the Greek but, again, who are we talking about, and why then bother to push him off the *Facciatone*? I feel like I'm just going around in circles.' He sounded as bemused and frustrated as I felt.

'Of course, there's still the Thomas scenario: what if Diamantis was murdered by Thomas Cartwright in a fit of rage after being accused of plagiarism, so as to safeguard his reputation? We now know that Thomas was already furious as a result of his spat with his boyfriend, Peter Fowler. Fowler has told us that he saw Santini walking about that night, so maybe when Thomas slipped out and murdered Diamantis, Santini saw him do it and as a result Thomas – or even his lover, Peter Fowler – decided to murder him yesterday to get rid of the only witness?'

Bruno groaned. 'I'm going to have to sit down and talk to the four of them again.'

'Definitely. By the way, I noticed something interesting last night.' I went on to tell him about the little heart-shaped pendant hidden way down Freja's cleavage. 'I suggest you ask her about it. Of course, it may be quite innocent – a love token from her occasional boyfriend.'

'Or it might not be. If it was an expensive gift from Diamantis, who was murdered by Santini, then that increases the odds that Freja killed Santini. Presumably her relationship with the Greek wasn't as casual as she would have us believe, but how could she know that Santini murdered Diamantis? God, if only these scientists could just concentrate on saving the planet...' Bruno ran his hands through his hair in frustration. 'Anyway, the good news from your point of view, Dan, is that I've been provided with an official interpreter today so you go off and enjoy yourself. Why not take Virgilio and Lina with you? You've been a great help and I really appreciate that, but you're supposed to be on holiday. Take it easy.'

'If you're sure, then, yes, that's what we'll do, but you will keep me informed of developments, won't you?'

* * *

Anna and I met up with the other two at breakfast and we agreed that we would make the visit to the sword in the stone that should have happened on Saturday. The sky was beginning to clear as we set off for San Galgano, but the atmosphere in the car was still a bit strained. Whether this was to do with the two murders or the ongoing tension between Virgilio and his wife was hard to tell, but Anna did a great job, launching once more into tourist-guide mode as she pointed out places of interest along the way.

The scenery around here was quite different from the area where I lived, closer to Florence. Although there were vineyards and some olive groves, there were numerous patches of dense woodland where I could well imagine packs of wolves living happily, preying on rabbits, pheasants, deer and occasional chickens or lambs stolen from the locals. We were soon on minor roads that twisted and turned as they climbed and then descended the hills, and from time to time we came across villages that probably hadn't altered very much since the Middle Ages. The houses and churches were mostly built of stone, the window surrounds finished with the traditional sun-bleached bricks that had withstood all weathers for half a millennium or more. With Anna's running commentary, it was easy to imagine knights on horseback, aristocratic ladies in wimples and, of course, desperately poor countryfolk trying to scrape a living in the fields. As always, Tuscany worked its magic on me, evoking an immense feeling of history, and I even managed to forget about the murders for a while.

It took barely half an hour to get to our destination. As we drove up the road leading to the abbey, we began to see cars parked on the verges and between the cypress trees. Quite clearly we weren't going to be the only people here today. We drove past the impressive façade of the abbey and parked in our turn just as the road narrowed and started to climb towards the unusual circular chapel where the sword was reputed to lie. We walked the short distance up to the chapel from where there was a fine view out over open fields, rows of vines and, as always, that typical Tuscan mix of cypress trees and umbrella pines.

My enjoyment of this tranquil scene, which might well have been why the hermit Saint Galgano had chosen this spot over eight hundred years earlier for his home, was rudely interrupted when Oscar spotted a couple of scrawny, black and white cats. I didn't have him on a lead and I had to chase after him, shouting commands that he completely ignored, until I was able to grab his collar and pull him away from where the cats had taken refuge on top of a wall. They looked on disdainfully as I gave him a telling-off and led him back to the chapel where he and I waited until the others came out again before I could leave him with Anna and take my turn to go inside.

It was just as well that I didn't go in there with Oscar as the overwhelming first impact as I walked into the interior with its perfectly round ceiling was an overpowering reek of cat pee. I don't think he would have been best pleased. No doubt the cats we had just seen, along with all their friends and neighbours, had been making a habit of using the place as a feline convenience. Still, ignoring the olfactory assault, it was a weird and wonderful place.

Built in the twelfth century, the ceiling of the hermitage was composed of a hypnotising series of circular rows of red bricks interspersed with strips of white plaster, almost like a massive target or being inside one of the mint humbugs my grandma used to give me. In the middle of the floor, protected by a solid, transparent, plastic case, was an outcrop of rock, or possibly a buried boulder, with the handle of a rusted steel sword protruding from it. According to Anna, this was a genuine early medieval artefact, and numerous attempts had been made over the years to remove it, but without success. In the car, she had told us that any number of legends surrounded it, not least the one that had distinct *Indiana Jones* overtones as it claimed successful removal of the sword would lead the bearer to the Holy Grail. Whatever the truth of it, it was an impressive sight and it only added to the other-worldly feeling of the place. As I looked at it, I shivered, but that might just have been the fact that it was damp and cold in there.

I was quite glad to get outside again and the four of us strolled back down the hill towards the ruined abbey itself. As we did so, Lina made an observation that stopped me in my tracks.

'Seeing that sword in there made me think of something. You know you told us that Bruno said the man in Siena was stabbed with a stiletto before being pushed over the parapet – well, I've just had an idea.' She must have seen the surprise on her husband's face as well as mine when we heard her volunteering information about a police investigation. I took heart from this. Maybe this signified that she wasn't going to present Virgilio with the ultimatum I had faced at the end of my marriage: my wife or my job.

'Go on, then, let's hear it.' Virgilio sounded intrigued.

'If I've understood correctly, one or more of your suspects is a woman, isn't that right?' We both nodded and she continued. 'You said that the man was stabbed with a long, thin weapon and it occurs to me that I've got something in my handbag right now which could probably produce the same effect. What do you think?' She stopped and opened her bag, rooted around inside it for a few moments before pulling out an aluminium comb. Unlike any comb I had ever used, this comb had teeth but it also had a long, thin, pointed handle as long as the comb itself and which no doubt served to remove tangles or to accomplish some other technical hairdressing task – I would never claim to be a world authority on coiffure. We all immediately saw what she meant. If somebody were to grip the comb by the teeth, they would have an efficient pointed metal stiletto about six inches long – long enough to punch through a man's back and pierce the human heart.

Virgilio and I exchanged glances and there was surprise and renewed respect in his voice. 'Lina's absolutely right. If the murder weapon really was something like this, it means that Santini's killing could even have been a spur-of-the-moment thing – and almost certainly by a woman – rather than a meticulously planned affair with concealed weapons involved.' He stretched his arm around his wife's shoulders and kissed her on the forehead. 'Brilliant, *carissima*, that's absolutely brilliant. Have you ever thought about becoming a detective?'

She made no reply but these few words got me thinking, not just about the murders. Lina was potentially looking for a job and Dan Armstrong Private Investigations was sorely in need of a new member of staff. Now that was a thought...

We went for lunch in nearby Chiusdino. This little town was perched on a hilltop and the views were splendid, especially through the panoramic windows of the restaurant. We were given a table by a large picture window from where we looked out over the southern Tuscan hills. The meal itself was traditional Tuscan fare and the mood around the table had lightened as a result of Lina's observation about the murder weapon. In fact, over *pappardelle alla lepre*, she came up with a question that had been preying on my mind as well.

'Do you think there'll be another murder?'

Virgilio and I exchanged glances and I left it to him to answer as I mopped up the last of the rich, gamey sauce on my plate with a chunk of bread. 'I suppose that's always a possibility. Bruno's been unable to come up with any link between the two victims as far as their work was concerned – one, a marine mammal expert and the other, a microbiologist – so it's looking more and more likely that there was a woman involved either as the murderer or as the catalyst to murder, rather than industrial espionage or some crazy person with a grudge. The question is, which woman? As far as we can see, there are two main female suspects: Freja Blomqvist and Monica Fowler. Take your pick. The Fowler woman has been open about her love for Diamantis but the pendant you spotted around Freja's neck would appear to show that she was also very close to him.'

I thought I should add another name to the list. 'It might be worth considering Carla Vespucci as well. She was asking after Santini last night, but she wouldn't say why.'

Virgilio looked dubious. 'Yes, okay, but would she appeal to guys like Diamantis or Santini? She's not exactly the most attractive of women.'

'There's no accounting for taste and, besides, Professor Pelletier said Carla had let herself go recently. Maybe in her former incarnation, she looked better.'

Virgilio still didn't look convinced but he nodded. 'So three possibles, and don't let's forget that there are another forty or fifty women in the symposium and, as already established, Diamantis was anything but monogamous. Alternatively, there's still a cloud hanging over the heads of Thomas Cartwright, who might have killed Diamantis out of professional pique, and Peter Fowler, who might have killed him because he was jealous of his wife's relationship with the Greek. But the complication is, who killed Santini and why? If the same person killed both men, then I suppose we have to accept that a third murder is indeed possible.'

'And if that's the case, there's still the chance that both murders were random killings by somebody with a grudge against wolves or scientists.'

'Which throws the local farming community back in the mix along with your weird Austrian guy.' Virgilio glanced over at his wife. 'What do you think, Lina? If Santini was killed by a woman, who's your money on?'

I concentrated on Virgilio and Lina, wondering how she would react to being asked to comment on police business. I could tell that he was apprehensive that, in spite of her interest in the case as shown by her suggestion of the comb as a murder weapon, that might have been only a one-off and I could see he was waiting anxiously for her reply, as was I. When it came, it was remarkably positive.

'I suppose I would have to say the English lady. I don't know any of those women very well, but you did say that she told you she was madly in love with Diamantis, didn't you? How about this as a scenario: Santini killed Diamantis and so the Englishwoman killed Santini in order to get revenge.'

Virgilio nodded slowly. 'You might be right at that. Of course, you could make almost the same argument for it having been the Swede, but maybe you're right.' He glanced across at Anna. 'What about you, Anna, what do you think?'

'I don't know Carla Vespucci well enough but somehow I don't see her as having sufficient motive. To be quite honest – and a bit bitchy – I agree that I don't think she's pretty enough to have appealed to either of the two men, who were probably a bit out of her league. Also I'm not convinced it was the lady from Manchester. If Dan's author friend Freja was wearing a love token from Diamantis – and worn so far out of sight as to be almost invisible to anybody without my boyfriend's X-ray eyes – maybe her feelings for the Greek were stronger than she's been prepared to admit. Wearing jewellery for ornamentation is one thing but wearing something but keeping it hidden is particularly intimate, to my way of thinking. My money has to be on Santini as the killer of Diamantis, but Freja as the one who killed Santini.'

Virgilio smiled at her. 'A very good point.' He turned his attention to me. 'And you, Dan? Do you have a detective's hunch one way or the other?'

'I honestly don't know, and I don't envy Bruno the task of building a case against either of them. The main problem with finding out who killed Santini is: if he really murdered Diamantis, how did his killer know he was the one who did it? Did they see him or did somebody tell them? Or did Santini tell them himself?' I reached for my wine glass. 'There are times when I'm glad I've retired.'

After an excellent lunch and a walk around the little town, we drove back to the hotel by a circuitous route, stopping off to visit no fewer than three churches, a ruined castle, the ruins of a

Roman villa and a gelateria with a wondrous selection of twenty-seven different flavours of home-made ice cream. It had been an excellent day and Anna and I were both secretly delighted to have found Lina sounding more upbeat and, indeed, interested in her husband's work. Back in our room, I mentioned my idea about there maybe being a place for Lina to work alongside me, and Anna was enthusiastic.

'Great idea, Dan. You need some extra help – you've been telling me that for weeks now – and Lina's sounding really interested in the investigation all of a sudden. Why don't you ask her?'

I wondered whether I should mention it to Virgilio first but, when all was said and done, it was up to Lina what she wanted to do so I decided to float the idea to the pair of them over dinner and see how they reacted.

17

MONDAY EVENING

I didn't see Bruno that evening but some of his men in uniform were still in evidence at the hotel, presumably carrying out further searches but no doubt partly there to reassure the delegates, who had by now been informed of the second murder. Among them was young Gori and he sought me out in the bar before the evening meal to give me a progress report from the inspector.

'The main suspects have been questioned once more but without any kind of breakthrough. Because there's no way of knowing exactly when Santini was murdered, since there are no witnesses to his fall from the top of the *Facciatone* and no CCTV footage, we can't even place any of the suspects there at the same time as the victim.' He shrugged helplessly. 'We've removed most of Santini's belongings for closer investigation but unless his laptop or phone produce anything interesting, we're still very much in the dark.'

'How did the people you interviewed this morning react to the news that Santini had been murdered?'

I was impressed that he didn't need to consult his notebook. 'The Swedish lady was visibly upset although she didn't actually cry. Monica Fowler didn't really react very much but she was looking stressed even before she heard the news of his murder.' He caught my eye for a moment. 'There was perspiration on her brow and I could see her twisting and turning her fingers nervously. She certainly didn't look comfortable. As for the woman with the specs, Carla Vespucci, she was probably the least upset of the three. Certainly none of them appeared too cut up about his death.'

'And the two men: Peter Fowler and Thomas Cartwright?'

'Pretty impassive, really. I couldn't see any change in expression when they heard that Santini had been murdered. Word has obviously got round that we believe Santini murdered Diamantis, but none of the people we interviewed could offer any suggestions as to who might have killed either man.'

'Did the inspector ask Freja Blomqvist about the pendant she wears?'

'Yes, she pulled it out and showed it to us and it was just like you said and exactly like the one on the note found in the waste bin. She said it was a present from Diamantis but, to be honest, she didn't appear particularly embarrassed or concerned that we were asking about it. If she had been the one to write the note luring him into the garden, I would have expected more reaction, so who knows? What she did say was that Diamantis told her to keep it hidden, as a secret symbol of his affection. That's why she has it on such a long chain – for her eyes only… and his.'

* * *

Dinner that night was memorable, but not just for the wonderful fish stew served with roast fennel sprinkled with parmesan. Virgilio and Lina were looking and sounding more settled and the mood around the table was more cheerful – in spite of the thought that we might be sharing the dining room with at least one murderer, maybe two.

Towards the end of the meal, we were interrupted by an unexpected visitor. He was a tall, statesmanlike, elderly gentleman with immaculate silver hair, and even I could see that the suit he was wearing had been tailor-made. A perfectly ironed, white shirt and a dark-blue tie with a crest of a lion rampant on it completed the overall impression of affluence. Along with him was the hotel manager, who performed the introductions.

'Good evening, may I present to you the owner of the hotel, the Marquis of San Bartolomeo?'

Virgilio and I stood up and shook hands with the marquis. Oscar also got to his feet and started wagging his tail, quite possibly in the hope of getting food from the new arrival. The marquis looked down indulgently and ruffled his ears. 'A fine-looking Labrador. Who does he belong to?' When I indicated that I had that privilege, he gave me a little smile. 'My old Labrador died last year and I haven't had the heart to replace him yet. Seeing your dog reminds me that I need to move on and get myself a replacement.' Seeing us still standing, he motioned us back to our seats.

'Do sit down, gentlemen.' His accent was as patrician as his bearing. 'I understand that you've been kind enough to assist the Siena police in investigating this awful murder.' His use of the singular indicated that he had either not heard about the death of Santini or had dismissed it as of less importance as it had not taken place on his turf. 'I wanted to give you my personal thanks and to ask whether you would be able to join me when I welcome the symposium delegates to my home tomorrow evening for dinner. It's the very least I can do after you've given up your free time so generously.'

His expression became more bleak. 'It was my hope that this

would be a celebration at the end of a fruitful weekend of work for the delegates, and we had planned to have music and dancing as well. Naturally, under the present tragic circumstances, that will now no longer take place but I can at least promise you a good meal. Please would you do me the honour of accepting this little gesture of thanks?' He glanced down. 'And do, please, bring your dog. I miss having a Labrador in the house and I'll be delighted to see him as well.'

Virgilio thanked him and accepted the invitation on behalf of the five of us, after which, the marquis shook hands with us once more before moving off. As he disappeared from sight, Anna gave us an idea of what might be waiting for us the next day. 'Castel San Bartolomeo is reputedly a Renaissance jewel, but it's private and it's been strictly out of bounds for decades. Nobody from my university has ever been invited inside so I'm really looking forward to seeing what it's like.' She pulled out her phone and scrolled through until she found a photo, which she pushed across the table towards us. The castle, totally surrounded by dense forest, was quite unlike anything else I had seen over here in Italy. Its extravagant towers and spires reminded me of photos I had seen of Ludwig II of Bavaria's crazy Neuschwanstein castle and it definitely promised to be interesting. I just hoped Oscar would behave himself.

I took advantage of the more jovial mood at table to pitch my proposal to Lina and Virgilio. 'The way things are going, I definitely need somebody to help me in the office.' I glanced across at Lina. 'Somebody bright who has a good investigative mind. It wouldn't necessarily be the most glamorous of jobs and it would mean sharing an office with a Labrador who can have attacks of flatulence from time to time, but if you were interested, Lina, I think you'd be perfect for the job. Do you think that sort of thing might appeal to you?'

I sat back and awaited her response, shooting a hasty glance across at Virgilio, who was looking very positive. I didn't have long to wait. 'How very nice of you to think of me, Dan.' She was sounding enthused and it was good to see a beaming smile on her face again. 'That's really thoughtful, but do you think I'm the sort of person you need? Might it not be better to get a big, tough man who could help you with the difficult cases? Or at least somebody who speaks better English than I do, seeing as many of your clients come to you because you speak the language.'

'Don't worry about that. I've heard you speak English and you'll be fine at answering the phone and meeting and greeting clients. As for the muscles, I'm not looking for a bodyguard or an enforcer. I gave up that sort of thing when I left the police. No, what I need is somebody with a friendly face and a good brain who's prepared to sift through all sorts of records and documents and so on, as well as to man the office when I'm out and about. I think you'd be perfect.' I turned towards Virgilio. 'Don't you agree, Virgilio?'

I was relieved to see him nodding his head enthusiastically. 'That's a wonderful idea, Dan. Thank you so much.' He looked across at his wife. 'What do you think, Lina? Would you really like to join the world of detectives like us?'

Lina was positively beaming now. 'If you can't beat them, join them. That's really kind of you, Dan, it sounds like a fascinating idea.'

I leant across to shake her hand. 'I'll sit down over the next few days and work out exactly what the job might entail and how much I can afford to pay you but, assuming you like the look of all that, then welcome aboard.'

Virgilio stood up and headed out towards the bar. 'I feel we need a bottle of something fizzy to celebrate. Just give me a minute.'

Seconds after he had disappeared out of the door, our celebrations were interrupted by a gut-wrenching scream, followed by the sound of chairs being pushed back and raised voices coming from the tables occupied by the scientists. I saw Gori come rushing into the room and I jumped to my feet, told the startled Labrador to stay where he was while I followed the constable towards the epicentre of the noise and confusion. What we found there was sobering and I instinctively checked over my shoulder to be sure that Anna and Lina had decided to stay with Oscar. Fortunately, they must have done so and I was grateful for that, because this wasn't pretty.

One of the circular tables occupied by the symposium delegates still held part-finished plates of food and glasses of wine but the seats were now all empty except for a lone figure sitting bolt upright in one of the chairs. It was Monica Fowler and she was motionless. I pushed past Gori and the gawping scientists and made my way across to tap her on the shoulder. Her skin was still warm to the touch but I could feel no movement. I leant forward so I could see her face and was immediately struck by her wide-open eyes staring ahead of her. What was most striking was the look of abject terror in those eyes. I had seen many dead bodies before but such an expression of horror was unsettling in the extreme. I waved my hands in front of her. There was no reaction. A quick check of the carotid artery at her throat confirmed that there was no pulse. Monica Fowler was dead.

Her body was locked in a rictus that held her upright but, as I knew all too well, there was no way that rigor mortis was likely to kick in and create that same effect for a number of hours. The pathologist would know better, but it looked very much to me as if she had been poisoned by something that had thrown her whole body into spasm and shut her vital organs down, probably in a matter of seconds. I was about to turn away when my eye was drawn to a thin, gold chain around her neck. I hooked it delicately with my car key and pulled it up until I could see that there was a little pendant dangling from it: one with a very familiar design.

I straightened up and beckoned to Gori, checking the time on my watch as I did so. It was one minute before 9 p.m. 'Get the names of everybody who was sitting around this table and mark the positions of them all on a diagram. Got that? We need to know exactly who's been near her and make sure nobody touches a thing. Plates, napkins, glasses, handbags: anything on the table stays on the table. Get down on your hands and knees and check the floor beneath the table and chairs as well but leave everything exactly where it is until Forensics get here.'

I looked around at the scientists who until recently had been occupying this table along with the victim. They all looked shell-shocked and I didn't blame them. Sudden death has that effect on people. By now, I recognised most of the faces, among them the two Spanish ladies along with their friend with benefits, Green-grass the Irishman, and a very subdued-looking Freja Blomqvist standing alongside Pavel Havel. The only one who didn't look totally dumbstruck was the elderly Professor Pelletier and she came over to catch hold of my arm.

'She's dead, isn't she, Inspector?'

I nodded. 'I'm afraid so.' There was no point pretending.

'Was it poison?' Our eyes were drawn to the partially eaten plate of food on the table in front of the victim.

'It could be, but I honestly don't know. Maybe a massive stroke or some sort of seizure but she's definitely dead.' I spotted two other uniformed officers at the door and called them over, giving orders to contact Inspector Senese and the emergency services – although I felt sure there was nothing the medics would be able to do for Monica Fowler now. As they hurried away, I caught sight of the victim's husband standing by a nearby table, being held back by Thomas, and I went over to give him the news. His reaction was unexpected. He burst out crying and I had to physically restrain him from running across to the crime scene. Luckily, Violet the headmistress appeared at that moment and led him away with a maternal arm around him.

'The Fowler woman, dead?' It was Virgilio at my shoulder.

I drew him away from the crowd. 'Definitely, and, as far as I can see, she's been poisoned. One interesting thing: when I was checking the arteries at her throat, I couldn't help noticing that she had a pendant hanging around her neck. Guess what: a little heart with an arrow through it.'

'Well, well, Diamantis would appear to have had a marked lack of creativity when it came to choosing presents for his lady friends. Presumably, this conquest had also been told to keep it out of sight as their little secret.' He looked around at the mass of bewildered scientists in the room before returning his attention to me. 'I wonder how many other women have got one of his little tokens secreted upon their person.'

We stood there and stared at each other for a few seconds before he asked the questions that were rattling around in my head. 'So who did it and why? What is it with these people? Are they trying to kill each other off?' He sounded as frustrated as I felt.

'Peter Fowler's reaction was unexpected. For somebody who claimed to live a completely separate life from his wife, he was very upset. Do we think he still loved her and, if so, does that make him even more of a possible suspect for the murder of one if not both of the other men?'

'He doesn't have an alibi for Friday night and as far as we can tell, nobody can provide him with an alibi for yesterday afternoon in Siena. But that doesn't help us find out who killed his wife and why.'

'In spite of his tearful reaction just now, maybe he killed his wife's two lovers and then killed her.' The other big unknown reared its ugly head. 'Also, come to think of it, if Monica Fowler really was poisoned, how was the poison delivered?'

'My money's on her food, but let's see what the pathologist has to say.' He glanced across at me and raised a weak smile. 'Some holiday this is turning out to be!'

18

TUESDAY EARLY MORNING

Next morning started just like the previous three with a walk for me and my dog, except that today I decided it was time for me to turn the walk into a run. I try to run regularly and after the amount of food I'd been consuming recently, I felt I needed it. Even at seven o'clock in the morning, the temperature today was noticeably higher than on the previous days and the sky was already a stunning, bright blue. Oscar and I jogged up to the same bench and I sat down to check my emails. The very first one I saw was from Suzanne, my editor in London, and it was amazing.

She had sent me two pieces of good news: one was a screen-shot of the newspaper article in *The Sunday Times*. The editor had dedicated a full page of the weekend magazine to Jess's very flattering article about me and this included a frighteningly clear photo of me holding my whodunnit in my hand while alongside it was another photo, probably taken from the newspaper's records, of me standing outside the Old Bailey some years previously after securing a long prison sentence for a very unpleasant drug baron. The headline of the article was *Giving Up the Day Job: How one of the UK's most successful detectives swapped crimefighting for writing.*

'Most successful' was pushing it, and I hadn't realised how many wrinkles I had developed until I saw them all here in high resolution, but I couldn't fault the article. Jess had clearly read *Death Amid the Vines* and she sounded most enthusiastic about the book and about my decision to trade London for Tuscany. Oscar even got a mention. I read what she said out loud to him, but it came as no surprise to me to find he was far more interested in chewing the remains of an old boot he had unearthed from somewhere. I sent Jess a gushing thank-you email, telling her how grateful I was and promising to take her and her husband out for a slap-up meal next time I was in London. It was the least I could do.

Suzanne's other bit of news was even more exciting: apparently on the back of the newspaper article, the book had now soared into the top one hundred in the charts. According to her, I could now officially call myself a bestselling author. For somebody who only a month before had been an unpublished author, this felt completely surreal and I forwarded the email to my daughter. I knew Tricia would be pleased for me and I wondered for a moment whether she would pass this on to Helen, my ex-wife, but then reminded myself that whether she did or not no longer mattered. I sent Suzanne my warmest thanks and turned my attention to my other emails.

Among these was one from Bruno to both Virgilio and me, sending us a copy of the pathologist's report on Monica Fowler's murder. Donatella confirmed that it had indeed been poison but indicated that she and her colleagues were still doing extensive tests to discover its exact composition. Apparently it was not a common toxin although she reckoned that its effect would have been almost instantaneous. She believed it to have been a powerful neurotoxin and hoped to be able to come up with a name within a few hours. There were no signs of puncture wounds, so she said the poison had most probably been administered orally, although, depending on the exact nature of this compound, it might even have been transmitted purely by touch. Whatever it was, it sounded like something very unpleasant indeed.

Last night had been chaotic. Finding a dead body in their midst had totally freaked most of the symposium participants and I didn't blame them. As requested, Officer Gori had prepared a seating plan of the victim's table, which had contained eight people. These had been the two Spanish ladies, Greengrass the Irishman, Freja Blomqvist, Professor Pelletier, Pavel Havel, a Japanese marine biologist called Takashi Nozawa and the victim. Bruno had arrived with a squeal of tyres half an hour after the discovery of the body and I had helped him with the translating as he'd interviewed each of the people who had been on her table, asking the same questions of them all:

'Did you give the victim anything, particularly food or drink, and did you see anybody else give her anything?'

Excluding various hotel staff who had brought water, wine and food, nobody had claimed to have seen Monica Fowler receive anything from anybody, either from those sitting near her or other members of the symposium. The two people sitting on either side of her at the round table had been Freja Blomqvist to her left and Doctor Nozawa on her right, but how the poison had been delivered remained a mystery – for now.

Anna and I had talked it over before going to bed and we had both agreed that it didn't look too good for Freja. If, as the pathologist had indicated, the poison had been added to the victim's food or drink, then it cast a shadow of suspicion over those sitting nearest to her. Our other prime suspects, Carla Vespucci, Thomas Cartwright and the victim's husband, had been seated further away, close to the kitchen doors, so would have had less opportunity. None of the kitchen or serving staff claimed to have had any contact with the victim and it was looking very much as though it had to be somebody on the same table, particularly somebody sitting close beside her.

As far as we could tell, there was nothing to link Doctor Nozawa with the victim either socially or professionally. He was a world-famous biologist in his forties and he told us he had a wife and two children back in Japan. He spoke remarkably good English and he was clearly a bright guy who would probably have appealed to members of either sex, but nobody here had so much as mentioned his name as having any possible involvement with any of the three victims. Professionally, there appeared to be no overlap either, as Monica Fowler had been an entomologist specialising in bees and Doctor Nozawa's overriding interest appeared to be sharks, so any question of rivalry appeared non-existent. Freja the wolf expert and Monica the bee expert were also similarly distant as far as their professional lives were concerned, but the little gold hearts around their necks indicated considerable overlap in their private lives.

Anna had told me she wanted a lie-in, so I decided to extend my morning run. I had been getting a bit lazy lately so, to make up for this lapse, I set off again towards the top of the hill so as to get a view over the other side further into the heart of unspoilt Tuscany. The track was clearly regularly used, and not only by humans. Regular piles of horse manure and other less easily identifiable poo attested to a variety of animals using this as well as people whose boots had left footprints in the softer soil at the edges of the track. As we climbed, so the view broadened on all sides until we emerged from the trees onto the hilltop. I stopped for a welcome breather and, although I was sweating profusely, I was pleased to find my breathing unimpaired by the climb. I admired the view while Oscar drank deeply from a puddle beneath a massive oak tree.

The track continued down the other side through the same dense mix of deciduous and evergreen trees until it reached a narrow road that I recognised as the one leading to Reiner and Suzy's house. In fact, I could just make the house out on the far side of the valley beneath its protective canopy of umbrella pines, but it was too far away for me to spot anybody outside in the grounds. However, my eyes were attracted by a movement much closer to me. Roughly halfway between me and the road, I could see a horse wandering about in a little clearing, apparently happily grazing on the abundant grass in the shade of the trees. From his white face and jet-black body, it looked like Reiner's horse, Boris. What was strange was that although Boris was harnessed and saddled, there was no sign of his rider and from this distance, it looked very much to me as if he wasn't tethered. Had he escaped or had something happened to his owner? Although the prospect of meeting up with the grumpy Austrian didn't fill me with enthusiasm, I called Oscar and ran down the hill to investigate. After everything that had happened, I wasn't taking any chances.

When we reached the horse, it was immediately clear that he was roaming free, but he obligingly allowed me to approach him and catch hold of his reins. I stood there for a minute or two, gently stroking his neck while I called out to Reiner or Suzy. When I received no reply, I began to feel decidedly suspicious. Yet another mysterious disappearance seemed like too much of a coincidence to me.

I set out to look for the missing rider and felt that the least I should do would be to take Boris back to where he belonged. As a complete numpty as far horses are concerned, I decided against climbing into the saddle as I probably would have ended up facing backwards or flat on my back on the ground. I gave the reins a little tug and, somewhat to my surprise, Boris let me lead him back onto the track I had been following, heading downhill towards the road. We had barely gone a hundred yards when we came upon his owner. Reiner was spreadeagled on his face at the side of the track, his arms outstretched, and the thought running through my head was that, just as I had feared, this might be murder number four. Hastily tethering Boris to a low branch, I hurried over to Reiner and knelt beside him.

To my considerable relief, I discovered that the man wasn't dead. He was, however, unconscious and there was a nasty cut and a livid blue bruise on his forehead. From the sand and gravel pressed into the wound, it appeared that he must have fallen off the horse face first and, without a hard hat, he had had no protection. The indications were that this had been a simple accident but at this stage, there was no way of knowing what or who had caused him to fall. The good news was that the cut had more or less stopped bleeding, so I decided to leave it to the emergency services to deal with. Very gently, I rolled him onto his side into the recovery position and, as I did so, he began to groan. I pulled up a clump of grass and used it to form a pillow for him. As I rested his head on it, his eyes opened and slowly began to focus.

'I know you.' There was a pause while he gradually got his wits about him. 'Why are you here? What happened?' He attempted to raise himself into a sitting position but it looked as if he was hit by a wave of pain and he subsided with another moan. I laid a comforting hand on his arm.

'Just take it easy, Reiner, and I'll call for help.' I pulled out my phone but before I could dial the emergency services, it occurred to me that I had no idea what this area was called. Anna had been the navigator the first time and I had just retraced my steps the second time. All I knew was that we weren't too far from the hotel. I glanced back down at the Austrian, who had closed his eyes once more. 'Reiner, what's the name of this place? What's your address? What do I tell the ambulance?'

I could see the effort it cost him to open his eyes again but when he spoke, he at least sounded lucid, if weak.

'Strada Provinciale 44, Podere degli Angeli. That's my address.' His voice tailed off wearily.

That was enough for me. I dialled 112 and explained to the ambulance people where I was and what had happened, and we agreed that I would go down and wait for them on the road. Remarkably, they indicated that the ambulance should be with us in twenty minutes, even though we were in the middle of nowhere. I was impressed – or at least I knew I would be if the ambulance turned up. In the meantime, they told me to try to keep Reiner from losing consciousness if possible. I checked my watch and saw that it was just after half past eight, so I settled down beside the Austrian and tried to get him to talk. Considering that, even before he had split his head open, getting him to talk about anything other than his burning hatred of scientists had been like getting blood out of a stone, I knew it was going to be an uphill struggle. I tried various topics until I hit on the subject of wolves and at the mention of them his eyes opened.

'Have you ever seen a wolf?' His voice was clear, if faint.

I shook my head. 'Only on TV, but I did hear one close to the hotel. What about you? I gather there are supposed to be wolves all around here.'

'There certainly are wolves here. I see them most nights.' Although still sounding weak, there was a degree of animation in his voice, which I interpreted as a positive sign. 'I sometimes sit inside the barn looking out at them through one of the narrow slit windows. I see them sniffing around the chicken run but it's well protected with wire netting so they can't get to them. The birds are obviously terrified and make a lot of noise, but they're safe enough.'

'I've been talking to some of the local farmers, some of your neighbours, and they hate the idea of having wolves anywhere near their livestock. What about you? Would you like to see them wiped off the face of the earth?'

He made another attempt to sit upright but once again was laid low by pain, and it was a couple of minutes before he found the strength to reply.

'Can I tell you something? I don't even kill a fly if I can help it.' That explained the fly curtain at his kitchen door, designed to warn them off. 'We're all animals with as much right to live on the earth as any other species. Why should humans feel they can hold the power of life and death over other creatures?' His voice tailed off and he lay back, closing his eyes again. I gave him a minute but then did my best to stir him again.

'So you believe in live and let live for all creatures, including wolves? But what if they start taking and killing your chickens?'

'They're carnivores, that's what they do. I protect my birds as best I can but, like I say, that's the way wolves are made.'

He didn't open his eyes so, in an attempt to stimulate a bit more conversation, I changed the subject to Boris the horse, who was contentedly munching his way through the remarkably lush grass at the side of the track. 'What happened? How come you fell off your horse?'

This did the trick and his eyes opened again. I noticed that his left eye, directly beneath the nasty cut and bruise on his forehead, was heavily bloodshot and I hoped this didn't signify internal bleeding.

'A porcupine.'

'A porcupine?' For a moment, it sounded as though he might

be getting confused but it soon turned out that such was not the case.

'A porcupine scuttled across the track in front of us and Boris shied. I wasn't paying attention and I fell off.' He winced. 'I don't remember anything after that until I looked up and saw you.'

One of the biggest surprise discoveries I had made here in Tuscany had been finding out that there were porcupines roaming the countryside. In my ignorance, I had assumed these were a more exotic animal to be found in far-flung places but no, Tuscany has porcupines as well as wolves, and that's official. It occurred to me that quite possibly there were experts on the subject staying in the same hotel as I was. Any further thoughts were interrupted as I picked up the distant but unmistakable sound of a siren approaching. I patted Reiner on the shoulder and saw his eyes open again.

'That's the ambulance. You just take it easy and I'll be back with the paramedics very soon.' To my surprise, he raised one hand and caught hold of my forearm.

'Thank you, you're a good man.'

Oscar and I jogged down the track to the road and were waiting there when the ambulance appeared around the corner. I flagged it down and went across to the driver's window. A bearded young man with a cheery smile greeted me.

'*Ciao*, how can we help? We've been told there's been an accident?'

Rapidly I explained about Reiner and his fall and offered to act as interpreter if necessary but the female paramedic alongside the driver reassured me that she spoke pretty good English. Just to prove the point she then asked me in English, 'Can we drive up to where he's lying?'

I had been thinking about that as I had run down to the road and was able to confirm that they should have no trouble. 'You'll see him by his horse. I'll follow you up with my dog and once you take over, I'll go and tell his wife – and I'll return their horse to them at the same time. Where will you be taking him?'

'To the *Pronto Soccorso* at Siena hospital. Do you know where that is? At San Miniato.'

I knew where Siena's Accident and Emergency department was located so I nodded and followed them up the track. As we walked, I looked down at Oscar. 'Well, dog, that was an exciting way to start the day, don't you think?'

In response, he deposited the stick he had been carrying by my feet. Evidently, to him, a game of fetch was far more exciting than some random man falling off a horse. I lobbed the stick into the trees for him, wondering idly how he would react if he came face to face with a porcupine.

19

TUESDAY MORNING

Oscar and I had a leisurely stroll with Boris the horse along the road and then up the drive to his home. I would have preferred to have walked faster but the horse clearly wanted to take his time and I was concerned that if I tried to gee him up, I might end up being outpaced by him. Visions of me desperately hanging onto the end of a set of reins belonging to a galloping horse didn't appeal in the slightest. I did say that I don't know the first thing about horses, didn't I?

Suzy appeared at the door in a paint-splattered overall as we arrived and I explained what had happened. She was understandably very concerned and I offered to take her to the hospital to be with Reiner. While she set about removing Boris's saddle and bridle and seeing him safely into a field, Oscar and I ran back to the hotel to pick up the van. When we neared the track leading up to where the accident had happened, I caught sight of the ambulance just pulling away, blue lights flashing, as it took Reiner off to hospital. I sprinted – well, ran quicker than normal – all the way home and altogether, it took almost an hour to get back to the hotel, give a drowsy Anna few words of explanation, pick up the van, and drive back to collect Suzy, but at least nobody could say I hadn't had a decent bit of exercise.

In the van, I gave Suzy as much information as I could about what I had seen and the extent of her husband's injuries, stressing that he had sounded quite lucid and would no doubt soon make a full recovery. She thanked me for my help and I turned the conversation to more general matters.

'I imagine it's at moments like these that you maybe regret not having a car. Do you feel the same way about modern machines as Reiner does?'

'To be honest, no, I don't. Yes, I appreciate and share his concerns for the environment and, indeed, for the survival of the planet, but some things are a necessary evil.' She gave a helpless shrug. 'Especially when we live way out in the country like we do.'

'Reiner told me you used to live in New York. Surely you must have had all manner of modern machinery and gadgets over there?'

'Of course, and we even had a car. Coming here was meant to be our attempt to get back to basics, back to a more natural lifestyle after corporate life in the big city.'

'What sort of work did you do, if you don't mind me asking?'

'I was a journalist at *The New York Times* and Reiner worked in the pharmaceutical industry.'

'The pharmaceutical industry?' I could hear the surprise in my own voice. I certainly hadn't been expecting this. 'I got the impression from what he was saying that he hates scientists. Does this mean he was one himself?'

She managed a little laugh. 'I'm afraid so. He trained as a chemist and spent most of his working life in a laboratory.'

'So why the dislike of science now? Did he have an epiphany?'

'Something happened, but he never talks about it now. They were doing clinical trials of a new drug and it all went horribly wrong. The drug had unexpected side-effects and three people almost died. It wasn't Reiner's fault but he took it really badly and that's when he decided he wanted to get away.'

That went a long, long way towards explaining Reiner's attitude towards science and scientists. An experience like that must have shaken him up considerably and I began to understand his desire to sever all links with the scientific world, although it couldn't have been easy on his wife.

'It must have been tough for you to give up what sounds like an interesting job and follow him.'

She shrugged her shoulders. 'What could I do? He's my husband and I love him.'

'Well, you've ended up in a gorgeous place. No regrets, I hope?'

Again that little laugh. 'Apart from the lack of power and heat, no, no regrets. As for giving up the day job, I keep telling myself that now I can concentrate on my art.'

I dropped her at the entrance to the hospital, gave her my number and told her to call me if she needed collecting. She thanked me and told me not to worry. When Reiner was released, she would make sure they travelled home by taxi – irrespective of any objections he might produce.

On my way back to the hotel, I called Anna to let her know in more detail what had happened. At the end of our conversation, I couldn't help voicing the thought still going round and round in my head since talking to Suzy. 'If Reiner was a chemist, then he would be ideally placed to know the best poisons to use if he wanted to kill somebody.'

'Yes, but only Monica from Manchester was poisoned. What about the other two? Besides, apart from his irrational hatred of scientists, what possible motive could he have had?'

'I'm coming around to thinking that each of the three victims must have been killed by a different person. If that's the case, I agree that it's highly unusual but I can't see any viable alternative. Maybe Reiner was murderer number three and he only killed Monica, but I know what you mean about the lack of motive. Anyway, I'll be home in twenty minutes or so. I hope they're still serving breakfast.'

It was only after ending the call that I remembered I hadn't given her the good news about my book being a bestseller so I immediately called her back and she sounded a whole lot happier for me than Oscar had been – but she wasn't chewing a boot.

By the time I got back to the hotel, they had finished serving breakfast but Adelaide, the friendly receptionist, was very sympathetic when I told her why I had been delayed and she led me through to the dining room to sort me out with some food. It was while I was standing by the observation window that separated the dining room from the kitchen, watching the team of chefs beginning preparations for lunch, that a thought struck me. When the receptionist came back carrying a tray for me with a large cappuccino, orange juice, fruit salad and a basket of bread and croissants, I thanked her warmly and told her what was on my mind.

'How do the chefs manage when you have guests who suffer from allergies?'

'You know that form you filled in when you got here? Didn't you see the question about allergies?'

'To be honest, I didn't fill one in. It must have been done for me by my friend who made the booking, but that sounds very organised. Right, so you ask people if they have allergies and then what happens? Say I was allergic to dairy produce or peanuts, for instance?'

By this time, it was common knowledge around the hotel that I was involved with the murder investigation and Adelaide was very obliging. 'Any allergies are noted and the chefs are instructed accordingly. Give me a moment and I'll ask Lorenzo if he can spare us a minute or two to explain.'

While I sat down to have my breakfast with my ever-hungry dog resting his nose on my lap and repeatedly licking his lips, just in case I didn't get the message that he was also looking forward to some breakfast, the receptionist disappeared back into the kitchen again. She emerged a minute later with the head chef. I hadn't spoken to him before but I recognised his face. He came across and we shook hands. Adelaide must have already briefed him and he was quick to explain the process they followed.

It was simple but effective. Briefly, guests with dietary problems were given a light blue napkin instead of the green and yellow napkins given to all the others. When food was served, waiters received instructions to ensure that the right dish was served to the appropriate client. He asked if I would like to see the list of guests with special dietary needs and I told him I was keen to do so, wondering if my hunch might pay off. He returned to the kitchen and moments later, one of his younger staff members came out carrying a clipboard. The list contained about twenty names and I scanned down it eagerly, almost yelling out loud when I spotted the name I had been searching for:

Monica Fowler Room 22 – *Crustaceans. No prawns.*

I queried with the sous-chef how alternative dishes were distributed until I had a good idea of the mechanics of what at first sight appeared to be a fool proof system and as soon as I had finished my breakfast – and had given half a bread roll to Oscar – I hurried out to see if I could find Bruno or Virgilio. I found both of them together, sitting at the far end of the bar, drinking coffee. Bruno greeted me with an update.

'*Ciao*, Dan, I gather you've been doing your Good Samaritan act with our Austrian friends. Some good news: I've just had a call from the lab in Siena. After Lina's suggestion about the comb, I got my people in Siena to do a search of all waste bins within two hundred metres of the *Facciatone*. I told them to look specifically for a comb with a long, thin handle and they found one last night in a bin at the corner of Piazza del Campo: made of aluminium, very sharp and definite traces of dried blood on it. The message I've just had from Donatella is that the blood belonged to Santini and when she compared a hair found trapped in the comb with the hair of the most recent victim, Monica Fowler, she got a perfect match. Lina was right. Santini was killed with that comb and there's no doubt about it now, he was killed by Monica Fowler. She stabbed him with the comb she was carrying and tipped him over the edge, hoping to make it look like suicide.'

'So Monica Fowler killed Santini...' I slowly digested the news, conscious of the two detective inspectors studying me closely. 'I must say that I believed her when she told us she was in love with the first victim, Diamantis, so I don't think she was involved in killing *him*. It's almost certain that the Greek was murdered by Santini so this must have been Monica's revenge. Would you guys agree with that?'

Bruno nodded. 'That's the conclusion we've come to, and now that we know that Santini was killed by Monica Fowler, we feel sure that she must have done it because he killed the man she loved.'

This all sounded very plausible but it didn't answer the question of who had killed Monica Fowler. 'If we assume that the first murder was a crime of passion then it's logical to assume that both of the other two were similarly crimes of passion, linked to the first.' A waitress came past and I quickly asked for another cappuccino and waited until she had gone off before continuing. 'Can I take it that we now accept that the murders were committed by people here, and our suspicions of some kind of anti-wolf conspiracy or an outside agency no longer stand?'

This time Virgilio answered. 'Definitely crimes of passion, nothing to do with wolves or any other animals.'

'And do we think Monica was murdered? Might she have committed suicide now that the love of her life was dead and she had killed his killer?'

Bruno and Virgilio shook their heads in tandem and Virgilio replied. 'We've been talking about this, but why do it there in the middle of a meal among a hundred other people? It makes no sense. No, she was murdered all right.'

Bruno nodded in agreement and then asked the obvious. 'Definitely, but even if we're pretty sure about who killed the two men, we still have to answer the question of who killed Monica Fowler and why.'

I had a horrible feeling I knew the answer to this one but I was loath to voice it. While I was still debating what to say, Virgilio came right out with it.

'How's this for a scenario? Santini's in love with Freja Blomqvist and/or Monica Fowler but he knows that Diamantis is involved with both of them. He decides to kill the Greek to clear the field. Monica Fowler, who loved Diamantis dearly, finds out what Santini's done and kills him in revenge. Freja Blomqvist, although she told us she wasn't interested in Santini, was really in love with him after all. She finds out that Monica has killed him and so she kills Monica for what she's done. Let's face it, she was sitting right next to the woman so she had ample opportunity to spike her food or drink with poison. For my money, the Swede did it.'

'Dan, what do you think?' Bruno looked across at me and I waited until the waitress had brought me my cappuccino before replying.

'There are a couple of tricky questions to be answered first. How did Monica Fowler find out that Santini had killed Diamantis, and how did Freja find out that Monica killed Santini?' A ready reply wasn't forthcoming so I carried on. 'I'm guessing that Peter Fowler told his wife he'd seen Santini on Friday night and that's how she worked it out. Maybe she then confronted Santini about it up on top of the *Facciatone*. Monica told me she had had other lovers apart from Diamantis and when I specifically asked her if any of them were here, there was a guilty pause before she said no. According to Peter Fowler, Santini and Monica have hooked up over the past few years so when they were in Siena on Sunday, Santini probably admitted or even boasted about what he'd done, and so she stabbed him. As for why Monica was then murdered, the simplest explanation is that somebody saw her do it and killed her out of revenge. Freja maybe? Or maybe somebody else who lusted after Santini?'

'Such as who? Nobody else had motive, surely?' Virgilio wasn't letting go of his Freja theory.

'Carla Vespucci maybe, who knows? She did ask me about him that time, but Gori said she didn't look too bothered about his death. She and Santini are both Italian after all, so they probably met up quite often.' I knew I was sounding hopeless. 'Or maybe it was one of the other women here at the symposium. How many are there? Forty, fifty? It's clear that Diamantis spread his favours liberally.'

Bruno didn't look convinced, but then neither was I completely, but maybe I was just clutching at straws to avoid the inevitable conclusion that Freja Blomqvist, aka Uncle Jack, was a killer. As I reached for my coffee, I moved onto why I had come looking for the two detectives. 'Anyway, although I'm still not sure *why* Monica Fowler was killed, I think I might have discovered *how* she was killed.' Seeing the immediate interest on both faces, I offered my idea.

'Last night, the main course was fish stew – and very nice it was too – but I've just discovered that the hotel knew that Monica Fowler was allergic to prawns and I can distinctly remember finding a couple in my stew. I asked what alternative they provided for her, and the sous-chef told me they had made a special batch without crustaceans for her and one other person with the same problem. Do you have a photo of the murder scene?'

Bruno opened the file on the table in front of him and shuffled through a sheaf of photos until he found a handful of shots of the dinner table with Monica Fowler's paralysed body still rooted to her chair. I checked what was in front of her and gave a grunt of satisfaction. 'See that: she has a different coloured napkin from the others. That told the serving staff that she had an allergy so she would be getting something different – in her case, something without prawns in it.'

'That's all well and good, Dan, but there's just one problem: presumably the other person with a prawn allergy ate their food with no ill effects, so how was the poison specifically put into her fish stew?' Bruno sounded impressed but puzzled. 'Does that mean that somebody in the kitchen or one of the serving staff put in the poison?'

'That's a possibility, but there's a simpler explanation. The sous-chef told me the special dishes for people with allergies are laid out on a separate table just outside the main door to the kitchen, and serving staff collect them from there. Each has a specific table number on it. She was on table seven and the other guest with the prawn allergy was on table two. If somebody was keeping an eye out for when the plates emerged from the kitchen it wouldn't have been difficult for him or her to brush past and squeeze a few drops of a very powerful poison into Monica's stew before the serving staff whisked the plates away. By the way, any idea exactly what sort of poison it was?'

'Donatella told me she should have an answer by lunchtime.' Bruno glanced at his watch. 'So, if all goes well, we should know in an hour or two. It certainly sounds as though you've found how the poison was added to her food. Annoyingly, this makes it less likely that either of the people sitting alongside the victim was responsible. I was getting quite excited at the thought that we might have found our killer in Freja Blomqvist, just like Virgilio said, not least because she was sitting so close to the victim. Now I'm not so sure.'

Virgilio frowned. 'I still reckon she's our best hope. Santini kills Diamantis, Monica Fowler kills Santini, so Freja Blomqvist kills Monica because she was secretly in love with Santini.'

I still wasn't satisfied but, in fairness to Virgilio, I couldn't really see any of the other potential suspects being any more likely. I sounded a note of caution. 'The fact is that, unless she confesses, you haven't got enough evidence to build a case.'

Bruno nodded morosely. 'Dead right, Dan, dead right. Well, I'll haul in Freja Blomqvist, Peter Fowler, Carla Vespucci and Thomas Cartwright and go through everything all over again.' He looked up and caught my eye. 'It's all right, the interpreter's arriving any minute now so you're in the clear. Besides, I know you're friends with Blomqvist so I'm sure you wouldn't want to be involved anyway. I'll be as tough as I can with each of them but I'm not holding my breath.'

I gave him a sympathetic smile. I knew only too well how it felt to be in his position – so near and yet so far from a conclusion to a case.

20

TUESDAY AFTERNOON

As the atmosphere in the hotel was understandably anything but cheerful, the four of us decided to go out for lunch. The fact that there was almost certainly a killer at the hotel, armed with some highly toxic – if currently unidentified – poison, added to our desire to get away. Anna and Lina had been talking to people in the spa and had heard about a restaurant in nearby Pontenuovo where the food was reputed to be excellent, so Virgilio and I agreed that it seemed like a sensible choice.

The restaurant was simply called Da Nello and if we hadn't known it was there, we would probably have walked straight past it. It was tucked away down a narrow alley close to the very old stone bridge that had once been the new bridge that had given its name to the town. This was the first time I had visited Pontenuovo, although I now knew what the mayor looked like – gigantic. His town, on the other hand, was anything but gigantic. It was a pretty little place, probably only half the size of my adopted home town of Montevolpone, and it had an impressive church, which Anna's expert's eye immediately dated to the twelfth century. The doors were locked but we were able to admire the impressive carved stone archivolt – being with a history expert was broadening my vocabulary – above the front door. This represented the intricately carved heads of no fewer than twenty different saints with Christ in majesty in the middle. Considering that Pontenuovo was little more than an overgrown village, it was a remarkable piece of work.

The restaurant was almost full but Anna, ever practical, had phoned and booked a table and they had confirmed that 'well-behaved' dogs were welcome so I was hoping Oscar would heed the warning I had given him. I had never forgotten the time I had tethered him to the leg of a hefty wooden table while I went to wash my hands in a Florentine restaurant that I no longer frequent – for obvious reasons. Oscar had spotted a tasty morsel on the floor left over by a previous diner and the next thing I'd heard – even through the wall of the washroom – had been a nerve-jangling scraping as he'd pulled the table across the floor towards his target, leaving mayhem in his wake.

Although it was far from cold outside today, there was a roaring fire burning in the fireplace. The hearth itself was probably a couple of feet above floor level and it soon became clear that this was where our lunch was going to be cooked. There had been no sign of a menu when we came in and the waiter had merely arrived with a bottle of water and a bottle of red wine. Clearly we would eat what they decided we would eat, and that suited the four of us just fine. As we ate our way through an excellent salad of smoked duck breast, dried figs, quails' eggs and rocket leaves, liberally sprinkled with balsamic vinegar and scales of parmesan, the chef appeared and began to rake the wood fire until he could set a cast-iron grill with four legs on top of the glowing red embers. Onto this he proceeded to heap all manner of meats from little lamb cutlets to steaks the size of a King James Bible and coils of spicy sausage. He followed this up with sliced courgettes and aubergines and chunks of salty pecorino cheese.

It was a truly memorable meal and the conversation flowed freely. Since my offer of employment to Lina, she had been sounding much brighter and more cheerful and she no longer appeared to resent Virgilio and me talking shop. In fact, she seemed more than happy to join in. It was interesting to hear what the two ladies thought about the most recent murder and they were unanimous. They had no hesitation whatsoever in deciding that Monica Fowler had been killed by another woman as revenge for the murder of Santini and they felt sure they knew who that woman was. I listened closely as Lina outlined most succinctly the convoluted course of events that she believed to have taken place.

'Diamantis was sleeping with Freja as well as Monica. Santini was in love with Freja so he killed Diamantis because he believed Diamantis had taken her away from him. Monica was in love with Diamantis so when she found out what Santini had done, she killed him as revenge and Freja, who secretly loved Santini, killed Monica in her turn. Sort of a four-pointed love triangle. Can you say a love square?'

Put like this, it all sounded logical and plausible – up to a point – but I felt I should play Devil's advocate all the same, not least because, deep down, I still didn't want to believe that Uncle Jack was a murderer. 'What I don't understand is if Freja loved Santini, why was she sleeping with Diamantis? What proof is there that she did love Santini? She definitely told us otherwise. More importantly, how did she manage to ensure that Monica got poisoned food? The chef said that the plates of prawn-free fish stew for the guests with allergies can only have been sitting by the door to the kitchen for a maximum of a minute, waiting for a waiter or waitress to collect them before they got cold. When Bruno interviewed the guests who were on the victim's table, none of them remembers any of the others getting up and leaving at any time. On that basis, I tend to believe that the killer must have been somebody else, purely from a practical point of view.'

Virgilio looked across the table and gave me a wry smile. 'Don't forget that your Swedish friend was sitting immediately to the left of the victim. Who knows, a moment of distraction, a sneeze even, and in goes the poison? I tend to agree with my wife – not just because I always try to agree with my wife on most things.' His smile broadened. 'That's the secret of a happy marriage, you know.'

At that moment, my phone began to vibrate and I checked the caller ID. It was Bruno so I answered immediately. '*Ciao*, Bruno, any news?'

'I've just had a call from Donatella. Monica Fowler was poisoned as we thought. It was in her food but not in any of the other plates around the table. She was murdered with a very unusual poison called tetrodotoxin, TTX for short. I've never heard of it but she tells me it's considerably more toxic than cyanide, and total paralysis is almost immediately followed by death in a matter of minutes, if not seconds. The particular variant found in the victim was a mixture of...' I heard him turn the leaves of his notebook '... tetrodotoxin, histamine, taurine, dopamine and a whole lot of other substances. Ever come across TTX, Dan?'

'I've heard the name but that's all. What is it and where does it come from?'

'It's found in a number of fish, as well as some octopus and newts, but most commonly in a Japanese delicacy: fugu or puffer-fish. Apparently, gourmets in Japan pay a fortune for slices of the fish and they say that the taste gets better and better the closer you get to the poisonous part. The result of this is a number of poisonings every year. It's a bit like people here eating the wrong kind of mushroom. It can happen.'

'Japanese, you say...?' This was interesting, considering who had been sitting on Monica Fowler's right. I didn't need to say anything. It was clear that Bruno had already worked that out.

'Quite a coincidence, isn't it? I'm going to have a long, hard talk to our friend Doctor Nozawa.'

'Of course, I suppose any scientists dealing with fish might have been able to gain access to the poison. Come to think of it, Professor Grosvenor, the president of the society said she was a marine biologist, didn't she? Not that I have her pegged as a murderer.'

When the call ended, I told the others what I had just heard and we all looked at each other in silence until something struck me and I thought it worth mentioning. 'A rare poison like this isn't the kind of stuff anybody would carry around for any other purpose than to commit murder. So whoever killed Monica Fowler came to this symposium fully prepared from the outset and with the intention of killing.'

Virgilio nodded slowly. 'Who could have loathed her so much that he or she came here specifically to kill her and why? Might our theory that Monica Fowler's murder was a crime of passion be wrong after all? Was she harbouring some deep, dark secret that had nothing to do with the other two deaths? Have we got it all wrong?' He gave a frustrated snort.

It was a good question and I didn't know the answer.

After lunch, we wandered around the little town for a while and had another coffee, sitting at a table outside on the cobbles at the far end of the square from the church. While we were there, we were approached by a familiar figure. It was Giorgio Carbonaro, the wine-making farmer. He recognised me and stopped to talk.

'Good afternoon. I hear that more of the scientists have been murdered.'

'Good afternoon, Signor Carbonaro. Yes, I'm afraid that's correct.'

'Wolves again?'

'No, not wolves, and the other victims weren't killed by wolves either.' I couldn't restrain a sigh of annoyance. 'Listen, the victims were all killed by *humans*. Do, please, get that into your head.' He still didn't look convinced so I spelt it out to him. 'One was hit with a club and mutilated with a beer bottle, one was stabbed and pushed off the top of the *Facciatone*, and one was poisoned. Wolves may be clever animals, but they aren't that clever.'

I saw him register the information and I hoped that this time it would sink in, but I wasn't counting on it. I could still remember the shiver of primal fear that had gone through me when Anna and I had heard that real wolf call the other night. Oscar had heard it too and had reacted the same way. I could understand why many country folk weren't keen on having wolves in their midst.

After Signor Carbonaro had wished us a good day and gone off, we finished our coffees and returned to the hotel. It was still pleasantly warm and when Anna went up to our room for a rest, I took my ever-willing dog for another walk. While I was out in the woods, I got a phone call from an unknown number. It turned out to be Reiner, sounding *compos mentis* and, for him, remarkably friendly and even apologetic.

'I hope you don't mind my calling you. You very kindly gave your number to my wife and I just wanted to thank you most warmly for all your help this morning.'

'I was happy I could help. How are you? Are you still at the hospital or have you been discharged?'

There was a momentary hesitation before he replied and this time he was sounding positively sheepish. 'I'm fine, thank you. I was discharged an hour ago. Nothing broken, just half a dozen stitches and a headache. But, to be honest, we're still at the hospital. While we were waiting, one of the doctors noticed that my wife was looking anaemic and they've been doing blood tests on her. We're just waiting for the results now.'

I wished them both well and put the phone down. It would appear that Reiner was having to rethink his opposition to science and doctors, and I was pleased to hear it. Maybe Suzy might even end up with electricity and heating in the house yet.

Oscar and I were out for almost an hour and in that time, I did a lot of thinking about the recent murders. Who had poisoned Monica Fowler? Could it really have been Freja and, if not her, then who? In spite of the possible Japanese connection with the choice of poison, I could see absolutely no link between Professor Nozawa and Monica Fowler so, once again, the inevitable conclusion was that the culprit was looking more and more like being Freja Blomqvist. I remembered the photo I had seen on Diamantis's Facebook feed of her amorously entwined with him and it occurred to me that I hadn't checked the social media of the others. Presumably, Bruno's men would have done this, but I've always been one of those annoying people who prefers to do things myself, so when I got back to the hotel, I dug out the iPad and did a bit of searching.

I gradually worked my way through the different suspects without finding anything startling before returning once more to the original victim, Nikolaos Diamantis of the University of Geneva. As I scrolled through his Facebook posts, I passed the one of him with Freja and a bit further down, I came across a couple of photos of a formal dinner back at the end of August last year, eight months ago. In these, I saw him sitting partway along a large table with a glass of champagne in his hand and a smile on his face. Beside him was a glamorous woman wearing an alluring evening gown and glittering earrings, her hair curled up onto her head in a very appealing and elegant style. From the way she was looking at him, she liked him. A lot. I blinked a couple of times before it sank in. The slim, gorgeous siren sitting beside Diamantis was none other than dumpy Carla Vespucci, normally to be found dressed in a sack and sporting thick-framed glasses and a severe ponytail.

This was without doubt an important discovery. As far as I was aware, there had been no mention so far of any direct link between Carla Vespucci and Nikolaos Diamantis, although Professor Pelletier had indicated that there might have been a spark there – at least on Carla's part. From this photo, two things were clear: first, the two of them had known each other well and, second, this earlier version of Carla had suddenly catapulted her into the sort of glamorous woman who would have appealed to an inveterate womaniser like the Greek.

What did this mean? From the way she was looking at him in the photo, it seemed most unlikely that she would have wanted to kill him, but might she have wanted to kill Monica Fowler because they had both been in love with the Greek? But why kill Monica two days *after* the death of Diamantis when that no longer mattered? It was baffling. Had Lina's love square just got a new corner? Had Carla replaced Freja or were we now dealing with a pentagon? I ran through it in my head: Santini killed Diamantis, Monica killed Santini and could it have been Carla or Freja who killed Monica? But the big unknown was still why?

21

TUESDAY EARLY EVENING

I met up with Virgilio in the bar at six o'clock. He was wearing a suit and looking very smart in readiness for the dinner party at the marquis's castle. I was also wearing a suit and silently thanking Anna for having bullied me into bringing it in spite of my objections. She had managed to find a brush and as a result, even my dog was gleaming. Around us, the scientists were beginning to assemble in readiness for the arrival of the coaches to take them to Castel San Bartolomeo although, understandably, the mood was far from festive.

Virgilio had been talking to Bruno and he gave me an update.

'Bruno says he's grilled Nozawa, Blomqvist, Fowler, Cartwright and Vespucci but without getting anything that would stand up in a court of law. He's taken their passports and told them they'll be interviewed under oath at Siena *questura* tomorrow morning but, between you and me, he's not that hopeful. He said the Japanese guy was very convincing in saying that he had no hand in it and that, although he said he was aware of the toxic properties of TTX, there's no way he would have been allowed to bring something like that from Japan anyway. He told me it's such a powerful poison that even a tiny amount of it in a bowl of punch could kill everybody who took so much as a sip of it in minutes.'

'So where did the poison come from?'

Virgilio shrugged. 'Who knows? The others all continue to deny any involvement in any of the murders. Bruno told me he questioned the Vespucci woman after you spotted that photo of her at a dinner party with Diamantis.' I had phoned and left a message on Bruno's phone. 'He says thank you, but all he got out of her was that she and Diamantis used to be close – she insisted on the past tense – but that they split up a month or two before Christmas.'

'I wonder why that was. Was there another woman involved? Might it have been Monica? Did Diamantis dump Carla for Monica? Might that be a motive for murder?'

'I wondered the same thing and Bruno says he put that to Vespucci, but she continues to deny any interest in Diamantis. There's also the question of where she might have procured the poison. She was part of the pair who collected the society's prize on the first evening for their study of slugs, not marine life, so it's unlikely she could have got hold of it without asking somebody, and that might have aroused suspicion. So, for the moment, Bruno hasn't got anything positive against any of them, although my money's still on your Swedish friend.'

I ran into my Swedish friend at the bar when I was waiting to ask for a glass of white wine – or, rather, she ran into me. I felt a tap on my shoulder and turned to see her looking predictably lovely in yet another revealing dress, but this time, there was no cheery smile on her face. In fact, she looked as if she had been crying. She caught hold of my arm with both of her hands and gazed up at me pleadingly.

'Dan, *you* don't believe I'm a murderer, do you? The Italian inspector was really quite nasty this afternoon with his questions and he told me I'm being hauled off to the police station tomorrow for interrogation. I'm going to miss my flight home because he's taken my passport. I've told him all I know and that I had nothing to do with any of the deaths, but it seems to me that he's convinced I did it, and I'm terrified I could be caught up in a miscarriage of justice.'

She looked so vulnerable, I had to resist the impulse to put my arm around her and give her a cuddle, but I answered honestly. 'No, Freja, I don't believe you're a murderer and I'm sure that you've nothing to fear if you are innocent as you say. Inspector Senese is a good man and I trust his judgement. He's just trying to do his job and, as you can imagine, with three deaths in a short time, he's under pressure from all sides to get results.' I gave her what I hoped would look like an encouraging smile. 'Besides, from what I've just heard, you're not the only one. There are five or six people that he's going to be interviewing tomorrow, so try not to worry. Just tell him the truth and I'm sure you'll be fine.'

'Thanks, Dan, knowing that you don't believe I'm a killer means a lot.' She produced a tissue from somewhere and blew her nose. 'It's just so awful.'

Seeing her looking a little bit less fearful, I decided to see if she could help. Now that she knew she was being treated as a potential murderer, she might just be prepared to divulge information she had been hanging onto up till now. I led her out onto the terrace and along to the far end, well out of earshot of anybody else. 'Can you think of any reason why Monica Fowler might have been murdered? It's now clear that your friend Doctor Diamantis was killed by Massimo Santini and the police have evidence that establishes that it was definitely Monica who killed Santini. If that had been all of it, then the case would pretty much be closed now: two men dead, one woman arrested. The problem that the inspector now has is to find out who killed Monica and why. Have you any ideas?'

She shook her head helplessly so I tried giving her a little nudge in the right direction. 'Listen, Freja, I promise I'll help you as much as I can, but you need to tell me everything you know. You already said that you had a relationship with Diamantis but that it was just a physical thing every now and then. That's right, isn't it?' She nodded, so I continued. 'It's pretty clear that he was also in a relationship with Monica, but would I be right in thinking that she was also involved with Massimo Santini?'

'She had been, before hooking up with Nico. But as far as I know, she dropped Massimo when she and Nico got together – maybe five or six months ago.' She nodded to herself a couple of times. 'I'm sure that's why Massimo killed Nico. It was painfully obvious that he was besotted by Monica so when she discarded him so that she could be with Nico, he saw red.'

'But surely Santini was sniffing around after you, wasn't he?' I glanced down at my dog, who was also in the process of sniffing around, but in his case, it was for odd bits of breadstick that had fallen on the ground.

'He was and he wasn't. I think that was just a front or maybe an attempt to make Monica jealous. Certainly anybody could see that he was madly in love with Monica even if she didn't feel the same way about him.'

I mulled that over. At least that was now confirmation that my supposition that Santini had murdered the Greek because of jealousy for Monica had been correct. I carried on asking questions in the hope of getting more revelations from Freja.

'From what Monica told us, she felt that what she had with

Diamantis was serious. In fact, she told us she loved him. Does that ring true to you?'

She nodded again. 'Yes, that's what Nico told me. I think it amused him at first and it appealed to his ego.' She caught my eye. 'Although I found him very physically attractive, I was under no illusions as to just how much of a narcissist he was. I got the impression when I spoke to him alone on Friday that he'd decided that the time had come to spell out to Monica that all he was looking for was a bit of fun.'

'Do you think he spoke to her before he died?' After all, if he'd dumped the woman who had claimed to have been madly in love with him, that could have stirred up all sorts of emotions.

'No, I don't think so.' There was a long pause. 'At least, that's what I think now, even if I didn't at the time.'

'You're going to have to explain.' She was fidgeting nervously and I could see she had something on her mind so I pushed a little bit harder. 'If you want my help, you've got to be completely honest with me.'

There was a long pause before she finally took the plunge. 'The thing is, Dan, I didn't tell the inspector the whole truth. You see, I don't think Nico would have had the opportunity to say anything to Monica because he was in my bed that night until one o'clock in the morning.'

'One o'clock precisely? How can you be so sure?'

'It was just after one. I looked at my watch when he left and it was a quarter past. I'd been expecting him to spend all night with me and to be honest, I was pretty pissed off. He told me he had work to do – and it's true he was scheduled to chair a seminar next morning – but I must admit that I suspected he was going off to see Monica. That's the kind of thing that would have appealed to his ego – two women in one night. Who did he think he was, playing one of us off against the other and just leaving me like that? Of course, when I heard that he'd been murdered, I immediately thought Monica must have done it, but I didn't speak up because I knew I'd get caught up in the scandal and that would most probably get back to Björk, my husband.'

Presumably, Diamantis had left Freja and had gone back to his room, where he had found the note. At two, he must have gone out into the garden to meet what he thought was Monica without realising that the cryptic note had been written by Santini, who was out there lying in wait for him. 'So Santini killed Diamantis because Monica had dumped him in favour of Diamantis. When Monica found out what he'd done, she killed Santini for murdering the man she loved.' I caught Freja's eye. 'Right so far?'

'Yes, that's the way I see it too.'

'Which brings us back to my original question: who killed Monica? Any ideas?'

She shook her head slowly. 'I've been asking myself the same question over and over again. It makes no sense. As far as I know, Monica didn't have any other men, at least not at the moment. She's got herself a bit of a reputation over the past few years for sleeping around at events like this, so there must have been other men in the past, but I don't think there was anybody recently. To the best of my knowledge, there was only Santini and then Nico.'

'What about women who might have wanted to kill her? Can you think of anybody who might have had a grudge against Monica?' Seeing her shake her head, I offered a suggestion. 'What about Carla Vespucci? I believe she and Diamantis knew each other.' Something occurred to me. 'She works in Turin and Diamantis worked in Geneva, and it's not that far across the Alps to get there.'

Freja shrugged. 'I expect they knew each other, just like I know Carla because we meet at these sorts of events, but I never heard Nico mention her to me.' She managed to muster a hint of a smile.

'But then, if she was one of his conquests, he was hardly likely to tell me, was he? After all, in his eyes, that's all I was as well.'

There was an edge of bitterness in Freja's voice and I couldn't help wondering if beneath this vulnerable-looking exterior, there might also be a murderer. Who was it who said that thing about a woman scorned? I remember getting it wrong in a pub quiz when I said Shakespeare, but I couldn't remember the right answer.

I was still wrestling with my memory for trivia when Pavel Havel appeared at the French windows and beckoned. 'Freja, come on. The coaches are waiting.'

Freja reached up on her toes and kissed my cheek. 'Thank you for believing in me, Dan.'

I stood there watching her walk off and asked myself if that was true: did I really believe in her? Before our conversation, I genuinely had believed her incapable of murder but now an element of doubt had crept into my mind. After she had disappeared, I went back into the bar to find that Lina and Anna had joined Virgilio. He looked up as he spotted me. 'I'm assuming that your little tête-à-tête with Freja Blomqvist was business rather than pleasure.'

Conscious of Anna's eyes on me, I was quick to confirm that this was correct and I told them what Freja had just told me. Virgilio was still looking dubious but he made no comment. Instead, he finished his beer and stood up.

'The coaches will be leaving shortly. Are we taking your car, Dan?'

I pointed to Oscar, who was sniffing the two ladies appreciatively. 'I'm not sure how happy the bus driver would be if we took Oscar on the bus so, yes, let's all go in my car. Will there be any police there tonight?'

Virgilio nodded. 'Bruno has asked the marquis for permission to station some of his men at the castle just in case. He himself isn't coming but he's told me to call him at once if anything happens.'

We all looked at each other and Anna was the first to say what we were all thinking.

'Let's just hope there's not a fourth murder.'

22

TUESDAY EVENING

Castel San Bartolomeo was stunning. Unsure of the route, I followed the two coaches. The journey took less than ten minutes but by that time we were deep into dense woodland. The entrance to the marquis's estate was through massive, old, wrought-iron gates set into stone walls at least ten feet tall. A uniformed gatekeeper flagged us down but let us through as soon as Virgilio flashed his warrant card at him, and we drove up a winding drive until the trees suddenly gave way to a wide, open area, in the middle of which was the castle.

My first impression was that it wouldn't have looked out of place at Disneyland with its circular towers topped with crenelations, its ornate balconies and terraces, a mass of flags fluttering from flagpoles all around it and its host of leaded windows blazing with light. The modern coaches lined up outside it looked singularly out of place in a setting where glittering golden carriages would have been much more suitable. I parked out of the way over to one side of the open area and we joined the delegates making their way up a flight of stone stairs, wide enough to take half a dozen horsemen riding abreast. Oscar wasn't on a lead but, for now, he was behaving with unexpected decorum and, as far as I could tell, he had only nudged one lady's bottom with his nose so far and her reaction had been friendly.

At the top of the steps, a pair of liveried footmen were waiting to greet the guests and relieve them of coats and bags. Inside, we found ourselves in a huge, marble-clad entrance hall lit by the biggest candelabra I had ever seen in my life. I got lost counting the number of bulbs attached to it. Anna caught hold of my arm and led me down a corridor after the crowd until we reached a pair of spectacular carved doors, at least twice the height and width of normal doors. More footmen awaited us there and the marquis, in full evening dress, was waiting to greet everybody personally. We had to wait in line for several minutes before it was our turn and the marquis kissed the hands of Lina and Anna and bent down to give Oscar a similarly warm welcome. Fortunately, Oscar was looking slightly overcome by all the pomp and circumstance and he didn't jump up to kiss him in return.

'Good evening, good evening, welcome to Castel San Bartolomeo. I'm delighted you could all come.' He lowered his voice and leant towards Virgilio and me. 'How's the investigation going? Inspector Senese told me he's solved the first two murders but there's still the death of that poor woman to be resolved, isn't there? Any suspects?'

I left it to Virgilio to give the standard reply. 'I believe he has a number of suspects and he's proceeding with his enquiries.'

We walked into what was an enormous room with a wonderful herringbone-pattern wooden floor and more massive candelabras hanging high above us. A waiter approached us with a tray bearing glasses of champagne, water or orange juice, and we helped ourselves. I took a sip of champagne and looked around at our fellow guests. They were spread around the room in little groups, talking in hushed voices, quite possibly about scientific matters, although they were more likely discussing the recent murders. Among them, I caught sight of Professor Grosvenor towering above the heads of a little group, in which I saw Freja with, as always, Pavel Havel by her side. I thought back to that hint of bitterness in her voice that I had noted and for a moment, the thought occurred to me that maybe she and Havel were closer than we had been led to believe – close enough to be prepared to commit murder together?

A bit further on, over on the far side of the room, I spotted Doctor Nozawa, looking uncomfortable in a dinner jacket and bow tie, talking to Carla Vespucci. She was wearing a tent-like gown that did little for her appearance and it seemed barely believable that I had found photographic proof that only eight months earlier she had looked like a vamp. I didn't have time to study her at any great length as an immaculate footman appeared at my shoulder and addressed Virgilio and me.

'Gentlemen, His Lordship has asked if he can show you something. He thinks it might interest you.'

Intrigued, we excused ourselves from the ladies and followed the footman through a different set of doors, along a corridor and into a smaller room. When I say 'smaller' I should specify that this was still a lot bigger than all the rooms in my house put together. Evidently, this was the marquis's private museum and it was a treasure-trove of glass-fronted cabinets filled with artefacts ranging from Etruscan pottery to Renaissance brooches, marble and bronze statues, suits of armour, gruesome medieval weapons and stuffed animals. The footman led us to a cabinet where the display was a mock undersea scene where stuffed fish floated from silk threads above a pair of sinister-looking striped sea snakes and an amorphous brown and red blob of a fish that wouldn't have won any piscine beauty pageants, while a stuffed octopus peered out of a grotto at the sterile scene. Standing beside the display was the marquis.

'Excellent, thank you, Sebastiano.' The footman gave a formal bow and after he had retired, the marquis returned his attention to us. 'It's good to get away from the crowd for a little bit of peace. I thought you might be interested in this. In this display my father collected some of the most toxic creatures to be found in the sea – or, indeed, anywhere around the globe.'

He pointed at the ugly brown and red fish and elaborated. 'This, for example, is a stonefish and it's one of the most dangerous in the seas. The spines along its back are highly toxic and people who are unfortunate enough to step on them experience excruciating pain, which can often lead to death. The sea snakes are also highly poisonous but it's this fish I wanted you to see.' He indicated a grotesque puffed-up creature the size and shape of a small football. 'Inspector Senese told me that the latest victim was killed with TTX poison, and I thought you might like to see the fish that produces that toxin. This is a pufferfish, what the Japanese call fugu.'

As I stared at it I wondered how anybody could ever have considered eating something that looked like that. I've sometimes wondered what drove the first person to start smoking tobacco leaves or the first French peasant to sample frog's legs or snails – desperation, probably. The fish was truly bizarre, but so were its companions. I let my eye travel over the various horrors on display until I came to the octopus, which just looked like a small, multicoloured octopus. In its own way, it was rather attractive. I queried whether this was also poisonous and the answer was yes.

'This is the blue-ringed octopus and it's one of the most toxic creatures in the ocean and, just like the fugu, it's also one of a handful of animals that produce the same TTX toxin as the police told me was used to kill the lady scientist.'

Seeing as we were barely ten minutes from the hotel, I thought I had better ask. 'Are these stuffed animals still poisonous? Could somebody have had access to them?'

He shook his head. 'To the best of my knowledge, this cabinet hasn't been unlocked for decades and, anyway, I would imagine the exhibits are no longer poisonous. They must have been here like this for at least sixty years now so I would think that any toxicity would have long worn off.' He gave me a little smile as he bent down to stroke Oscar's head. 'But I wouldn't recommend giving them to your handsome Labrador to eat, just in case.'

Virgilio was still staring at the pufferfish. 'We've been struggling to work out how the murderer could have got hold of this toxin. Is it readily available?'

The marquis shook his head. 'Definitely not. TTX is on the list of the most toxic substances on the planet and, as such, possessing it is strictly controlled, and even in laboratory situations, people handling it take as much care as if they were handling radioactive material. Whoever got hold of it must have had high-level clearance.'

Once again, I thought back over the scientists whose chosen field of research was sea creatures. None of our suspects fell into that category apart from Doctor Nozawa, but I couldn't see how he could possibly have been involved with the murder of Monica Fowler. As for the others, Carla Vespucci studied slugs while Pavel Havel and Freja studied carnivorous mammals. But then the marquis added a detail that came as a bolt from the blue.

'There aren't many poisonous molluscs in the world, and thankfully you don't find the blue-ringed octopus anywhere near here.'

I stared at him blankly as my brain put two and two together.

'Did you say that this octopus is a mollusc?' Thinking back on it, I'd never been too good with the scientific questions in quizzes.

He nodded indulgently. 'Every single octopus on the planet is a mollusc. Why do you ask?'

'So somebody who studies slugs...' I searched for the technical description I had heard at the prizegiving on the first night and managed to come up with it '...gastropod molluscs, would also be involved with an octopus like this?'

'I would imagine so, but why the interest?'

Virgilio and I exchanged glances and he did the talking. 'We are indebted to you, *Marchese*, you may just have solved the case for us. Would you excuse us, please?'

The two of us, accompanied by Oscar, hurried back into the reception hall and stopped when we reached Anna and Lina to relay what we had just heard. As we spoke, we were both looking over the heads of the guests to see if we could spot Carla Vespucci.

'Suddenly, the Vespucci woman is looking like a far more likely prospect.' Virgilio was sounding as excited as I was feeling. 'We now know that she most probably works with the very poison that killed Monica Fowler.' He spotted Officer Gori on the far side of the room and waved to him to come over to us while he continued thinking through the possible ramifications of this discovery. 'How's this for a scenario? Carla Vespucci and Diamantis are an item up till last autumn, then he gets fed up with her and dumps her for Monica. Carla is heartbroken and vengeful so she comes here armed with TTX poison determined to kill the woman who replaced her in the Greek's affections. Sound right to you?'

'It does, but I wonder if Monica was her only target. Maybe she also intended to kill Diamantis, but Santini got there first. And, assuming she knew about Freja's occasional involvement with Diamantis, maybe she also intended to kill her... maybe she still does.' I looked across to where I had last seen Freja and was relieved to see her still talking to Pavel Havel.

At that moment, Gori appeared at our shoulders and gave a smart salute. Virgilio was quick to issue orders. 'We believe we have a lead as far as the murder of Monica Fowler is concerned. Make sure that you and the other officers guard all the doors to this room and make sure nobody leaves. Okay?'

I felt Anna grip my arm and saw her pointing with her free hand. 'Over there, Dan, it's Carla Vespucci.'

Sure enough, there was Carla, walking across the room towards where Freja and Havel were standing. In her hands were two glasses and I had a bad feeling as soon as I saw this. 'We need to get to her before she gets to Freja.' And I set off at a run, pushing my way through the crowd towards Carla Vespucci. When I reached them she was in the process of handing a glass of champagne to Freja and I was taking no chances.

'Give me that glass of champagne, Freja.' She looked up in surprise and I repeated the command, raising my voice. 'Just do it! Now!'

I took the glass from her, taking the greatest of care not to spill it, and transferred my attention to Carla as Virgilio and Gori appeared on either side of her. Using a calm tone, Virgilio indicated the door to the museum. 'If you would like to come with us, Doctor Vespucci, we would like to have a few words with you.'

Her facial expression gave nothing away as she obeyed stiffly, without protest. Gori and Virgilio flanked her as they marched her to the museum and I closed the doors behind us. Very carefully, I set the champagne glass down on top of the cabinet containing the poisonous sea creatures and returned my attention to her. She was still holding her glass of orange juice in one hand. I found myself focusing on that as Virgilio began to speak.

'Doctor Vespucci, would I be right in thinking that you are

familiar with an animal called the blue-ringed octopus?' In case she might be in any doubt, he pointed into the glass cabinet but she didn't bother to look.

'The *Hapalochlaena* family, yes, I study them.'

'Then you will know that they are highly poisonous?'

'Yes.' Her face didn't betray any emotion.

'Did you use that poison to kill Monica Fowler?'

Carla gave no reply and just stood there holding her glass. My eyes were still on the orange juice in it and suddenly, it hit me: she wasn't drinking alcohol. Her changed appearance from slim vamp to chunky, ill-groomed woman and her bitter hatred, not only for Monica Fowler, but also for the original victim, was explained. Diamantis had dumped her five or six months earlier. Why? Because she had given him some unwelcome news perhaps?

I leant forward to attract her attention. 'Tell me, Doctor Vespucci, when did you break the news to Nikolaos Diamantis that you were expecting his baby?'

I sensed a shiver run through both police officers. This question clearly hit home with Carla Vespucci and an expression of anguish crossed the woman's face. She still made no reply so I tried again, now confident that her physiological changes since last summer's photo had a simple and natural explanation: she was pregnant.

'You told him you were expecting his child last autumn and he left you for Monica, didn't he? Is that why you came here to kill her?'

'I came here to kill *him*.' She spoke so softly that all three of us leant closer to hear the words.

'With TTX poison?' I saw her give the slightest of nods so I continued. 'But Massimo Santini got there first.'

She nodded again.

'So when you couldn't have the satisfaction of killing him, you decided to take your anger out on the two other women in his life?'

'They deserved it.'

'And if we analyse the contents of the glass you just gave to Freja, we'll find TTX in it, won't we?'

There was the slightest nod of her head and then she raised her own glass to her lips and stared at me over the rim. 'And you'll find it in my glass as well. I have nothing more to live for.' Her voice was cold, emotionless.

Now all sets of eyes were on the glass in her hand, barely an inch from her lips. I spoke quickly. 'Don't do anything hasty, Carla. There's no need for that. Just think, you're carrying a child. You owe it to your baby to look after it... and yourself.'

The glass remained within touching distance of her lips and I knew that even the tiniest amount of the liquid would be enough to kill her. She was still studying me dispassionately as I tried again.

'It doesn't have to be the end of the world for you. Life goes on and you'll be bringing new life into the world. Yes, you'll have to be arrested, but that's as much for your own sake as anything else. Any judge will look sympathetically on your case after everything you've been through. Don't do it, Carla. Things will get better, I promise.'

'Things can never get better for me.' The anguish in her voice was palpable and I saw her fingers twitch as the glass moved a millimetre or two closer to her mouth.

A movement from the floor drew my attention. Oscar, who has often demonstrated that he is keenly aware of the moods of the humans around him, got to his feet and wandered over to lean against Carla's leg, raising his eyes towards her in support. I saw her look down at him and I was on the point of launching myself across to knock the glass out of her hand when she gave a little sob and lowered her glass while reaching down to stroke Oscar's ears with her other hand. Virgilio took the poisoned orange juice from her unresisting fingers and we all heaved a sigh of relief. I looked down at Oscar and couldn't help smiling.

He really is a very good dog.

23

TUESDAY NIGHT

'The power of love...' There was a melancholic note to Anna's voice.

We were taking Oscar for the last late-night walk any of us would be having here at the hotel. Next morning, we would be checking out and heading home, just like all the remaining symposium participants – including Freja Blomqvist – now that all the drama had finished.

I gave Anna's hand a little squeeze. 'Three deaths, and all in the name of love.'

Anna was still in reflective mood. 'Carla must have loved Diamantis very dearly for her love of him to have turned to such vehement hatred. But it wasn't just her. Santini must have loved Monica very deeply for him to go out and kill his rival, and she must have loved Diamantis just as much.' She turned towards me and I could see the bewildered expression on her face quite clearly in the moonlight. 'How is it that something so pure and so good can turn into something so ugly and evil?'

'If we knew the answer to that, half of my work as a detective would be wiped out overnight. I suppose it's like a pendulum; the

bigger the upward swing, the bigger the swing back down again.'
This was getting a bit depressing so I did my best to cheer her up.
'Who was it who said that thing about better to have loved and lost
than never to have loved at all? I know it wasn't Shakespeare.'

'Alfred Lord Tennyson, but I'm sure he didn't foresee lost love
turning so sour.' We walked on a few more paces before she
looked up at me again. 'How did Carla manage to put the poison
into Monica's food?'

'Meticulous planning. She found out about Monica's prawn
allergy and watched how the kitchen staff dealt with plates for
clients with special dietary needs. She chose a seat close to the
kitchen entrance, right beside the table where those plates were
laid out. All it took was a second or two to add a few drops of
poison. She probably hardly needed to get out of her chair.'

She nodded slowly. 'So she came here fully prepared to kill the
man she had once loved, her two rivals, and then finally herself
and the child she was carrying. How tragic.'

'And she would have done it, too, if it hadn't been for my four-
legged friend.'

The vineyards stretched out on either side of the track as we
walked up towards the trees. For once, Oscar didn't seem interested in playing fetch and he was trotting along between the two
of us, glancing up from time to time to check that we were all right.
I felt sure that he was fully aware that this evening hadn't been an
easy one for any of us. I don't want to come across as one of those
dog owners who reckon their dogs understand everything they
say, but I would be the first to admit that there's more to this
Labrador than just a dumb animal. I was bending down to give his
ears an affectionate scratch when I heard my girlfriend's voice.

'What's that, Dan?' The melancholy had been replaced by
apprehension.

She stopped dead and Oscar and I stopped as well. There was a rustling sound coming from the vines just a short distance ahead of us and I glanced down at Oscar. Even in this light, I could see the hackles of his back rise and I heard him give a low, threatening growl. This was so out of character for my normally docile pet that it worried me. Whatever creature was in there, Oscar didn't like it. I turned over in my head what sort of animal might be coming slowly but relentlessly towards us, its feet crunching on the dead leaves. If we were very lucky, it might be a porcupine or even a deer. What I didn't want to meet was a wild boar – they can be dangerous, particularly in the breeding season. And then, suddenly, the creature emerged from the vines, barely a handful of paces ahead of us, the dark shape showing up clearly against the light gravel surface of the track.

There could be no doubt about it. It was a wolf.

As it saw us, the big animal lowered its head towards us and bared its teeth – and there were a lot of them – and they glinted in the moonlight as it snarled at us. We stood motionless for what felt like an hour, but was probably just a matter of seconds before I began to react. Slowly and cautiously, I indicated that Anna should move back down the track towards the hotel. I then turned my attention to Oscar and was just reaching down to grab his collar when he took two steps forward, moving slowly and deliberately towards the wolf, still emitting that little growling noise. Although he's a big dog, compared to the wolf, he was small fry, and I felt sure if it came to a fight, he would be badly mauled. I took a step towards him but he evaded my outstretched hand and continued to approach the wolf.

I didn't want to get any closer to this potentially lethal wild animal whose savage growls had made the hair on the back of my neck stand on end, but I knew I would defend my best buddy. I looked around for a weapon of any kind but found nothing. I pulled off my jacket and rolled it around my right forearm just as

Angus the dog handler had told me to do years ago. He had been preparing me to meet a guard dog or a villain's mongrel, but neither of us in our wildest dreams had imagined I might ever encounter a wolf.

I saw a biggish stone at the side of the track and picked it up in my other hand while Oscar continued to advance slowly towards the very dangerous opponent. I had always thought of him as a fairly sensible animal and I couldn't understand why he was putting himself in such danger unless it was to protect me. All the more reason for me to be prepared to bail him out. I raised the stone in my left hand and was about to take a step forward when the most amazing thing happened.

The wolf suddenly stopped growling, sheathed its fangs and started making a plaintive whining sound. At the same time, I distinctly saw Oscar relax and his hackles begin to flatten. As I looked on in amazement, but still with trepidation, he approached the wolf and they touched noses. The immediate result of this slight touch was that I saw the end of Oscar's tail begin to wag. The wolf – and by this time I had worked out that this had to be a she-wolf – continued to make happy little whining noises as Oscar subjected her to a full olfactory audit, his tail now wagging ever more vigorously. As he got round to her hindquarters he looked back at me for a second and I swear he was grinning from ear to ear.

Slowly and carefully I retreated down the track towards the hotel until I reached Anna, who had witnessed the whole scene. She caught hold of me with both of her hands and held me tightly as she whispered in my ear.

'Aren't you going to call him?'

'I think the happy couple deserve a little bit of privacy, don't you?'

She grinned at me in the moonlight. 'Saved by Oscar once again.'

I smiled back. 'What was that you were saying about the power of love?'

ACKNOWLEDGMENTS

To my lovely editor, Emily Ruston, and the whole team at my exceptional publishers, Boldwood Books. Special thanks for the hawk-eyed copy-editing talents of Sue Smith and to Emily Reader, the proofreader with the perfect name. A warm thank you to Simon Mattacks whose narration for the audio version does so much to enhance the story. To my ear, Simon *is* Dan. Many thanks also to my friend, Elaine Brent, for being kind enough to read the original manuscript and offer her very helpful comments. Finally, a nostalgic nod to my beloved black lab, Merlin, who was the inspiration for Oscar.

MORE FROM T.A. WILLIAMS

We hope you enjoyed reading *Murder in Siena*. If you did, please leave a review.

If you'd like to gift a copy, this book is also available as an ebook, hardback, large print, digital audio download and audiobook CD.

Sign up to T.A. Williams' mailing list for news, competitions and updates on future books.

https://bit.ly/TAWilliamsNews

Explore the rest of the Armstrong and Oscar Cozy Mystery series...

ABOUT THE AUTHOR

T. A. Williams is the author of over twenty bestselling romances for HQ and Canelo and is now turning his hand to cosy crime, set in his beloved Italy, for Boldwood. The series introduces us to to DCI Armstrong and his labrador Oscar. Trevor lives in Devon with his Italian wife.

Visit T. A. Williams' website:

http://www.tawilliamsbooks.com

Follow T. A. Williams' on social media:

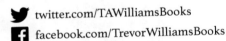

twitter.com/TAWilliamsBooks
facebook.com/TrevorWilliamsBooks

Poison
& Pens

POISON & PENS IS THE HOME OF
COZY MYSTERIES SO POUR YOURSELF
A CUP OF TEA & GET SLEUTHING!

DISCOVER PAGE-TURNING NOVELS FROM
YOUR FAVOURITE AUTHORS &
MEET NEW FRIENDS

JOIN OUR
FACEBOOK GROUP

BIT.LYPOISONANDPENSFB

SIGN UP TO OUR
NEWSLETTER

BIT.LY/POISONANDPENSNEWS

Boldwd

Boldwood Books is an award-winning fiction publishing company seeking out the best stories from around the world.

Find out more at www.boldwoodbooks.com

Join our reader community for brilliant books, competitions and offers!

Follow us
@BoldwoodBooks
@BookandTonic

Sign up to our weekly deals newsletter

https://bit.ly/BoldwoodBNewsletter

Made in the USA
Columbia, SC
24 September 2023